"So what does your brot
know each other."

"How many Wynns have you met, again?"

He grinned and conceded. "Only one, and that's on paper."

"So you *couldn't* know my brother."

Ha. Right.

Still...

"What did you say he does for a living?"

Teagan gave him an odd look, like *maybe drop this.* And he would, as soon as this was squared away, because the back of his neck was prickling now.

"Wynn works for my father's company," she said.

The prickling grew.

His gaze roamed her face...the thousand different curves he'd adored and kissed into the night. Then he considered their backgrounds again, and that *yet to be filed* libel suit. He thought about *his* Wynn, and he thought about *hers.*

Didn't matter. At least, it didn't matter right now.

Leaning in, he murmured, "That robe needs to go."

* * *

The Case for Temptation by Robyn Grady
is part of the About That Night... series.

Dear Reader,

I have never been more excited for one of my books to hit the shelves! Welcome to Teagan Hunter's story, the long-awaited final installment in a series that follows a goliath media family as they battle corporate enemies and assassination attempts that threaten to tear them apart. Of course, at the heart of each story is an even bigger, far more personal journey—one that challenges and changes each of the strong-willed Hunter siblings in ways they can never have imagined.

Teagan is her formidable father's favorite and the only Hunter determined to chart her own course. But Tea also has a heartbreaking secret that destroyed her hopes for lasting love. One sizzling night with a gorgeous stranger was only meant to be a distraction. However, New York lawyer Jacob Stone proves to be the man who could very well change Teagan's mind about *happily-ever-after*—if only he wasn't so hell-bent on bringing Hunter Enterprises to justice over a trumped-up, albeit serious, charge.

Secrets and loss, hope and, ultimately, a deeply deserving love. I hope you enjoy *The Case for Temptation*. Leave a review at your place of purchase and let me know what you think.

As always, happy reading!

Robyn

www.RobynGrady.com

PS: Search *The Hunter Pact* or *Sons of Australia: The Hunters* for linked stories.

ROBYN GRADY

THE CASE FOR TEMPTATION

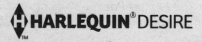

Recycling programs
for this product may
not exist in your area.

ISBN-13: 978-1-335-20888-0

The Case for Temptation

Copyright © 2020 by Robyn Grady

Printed in U.S.A.

Robyn Grady was first contracted by Harlequin in 2006. Her books feature regularly on bestseller lists and at award ceremonies, including the National Readers' Choice Awards, the Booksellers' Best Awards, CataRomance Reviewers' Choice Awards and Australia's prestigious Romantic Book of the Year.

Robyn lives on Australia's gorgeous Sunshine Coast, where she met and married her real-life hero. When she's not tapping out her next story, she enjoys the challenges of raising three very different daughters, going to the theater, reading on the beach and dreaming about bumping into Stephen King during a month-long Mediterranean cruise.

Robyn knows that writing romance is the best job on the planet and she loves to hear from her readers! You can keep up with news on her latest releases at www.robyngrady.com.

Books by Robyn Grady

Harlequin Desire

The Hunter Pact

Losing Control
Temptation on His Terms
One Night, Second Chance

About That Night...

The Case for Temptation

You can also find Robyn Grady on Facebook, along with other Harlequin Desire authors, at www.Facebook.com/HarlequinDesireAuthors!

This story is for Joan,
Teagan Hunter's biggest fan!

One

As the private elevator continued its climb to the hotel's presidential suite, Jacob Stone couldn't help but admire the woman standing beside him. Forget the *wow* factor of endless waves of silken blond hair. Her beaded off-the-shoulder number must have cost a small fortune, and on that body, it was worth every damn cent.

No one was breaking the law but, if put on the stand, Jacob would have to admit—there was way more than just looking on his mind.

Finally, she glanced across at him. "You know you're staring, right?"

"This'll sound crazy…" Lame even, but he'd put it out there. "This is a first for me."

"If you're saying you've never had anyone back for a drink before tonight," she laughed, "sorry. I'm not buying."

Jacob's teeth skimmed his lower lip as he propped a jacketed shoulder against the mirrored wall of the elevator and crossed his arms. This wasn't about a nightcap after the party. He'd be more specific.

"We've known each other three hours. Four max."

As her gaze eased away from his to the opening doors, one eyebrow hiked up. "Chickening out?"

His turn to laugh.

Not on your life.

Six weeks ago, Jacob had received a wedding invitation from an old friend, a lawyer who'd recently relocated to the West Coast. Marcus Lane had found The One and bought a ring. So Jacob had booked a first-class ticket from New York to LAX and attended today's extravagant garden wedding. After the ceremony, which ended with the traditional release of doves, he followed the trail of pinging crystal flutes to a ballroom more elaborate than any set from a Hollywood blockbuster. Impressive, and he was happy for Marcus and his bride.

But Jacob had been thinking more about the multi-million-dollar lawsuit waiting back home than being in the moment. Then this woman had appeared, seemingly out of nowhere, and his mind-set had done a one-eighty.

When she had stopped at his table, Jacob wasted no time getting to his feet and pulling out her chair. As wine was poured and introductions exchanged, he'd been struck by her eyes—the most sensuous, slumberous green he'd ever seen. He apologized when she'd needed to repeat herself.

Her first name was Teagan. He hadn't caught the last bit.

They'd been so busy talking that he couldn't recall

what they'd eaten or who had said what in a run of formal wedding speeches. And that juicy case back in New York? All but forgotten. After the bridal waltz, when the atmosphere dipped into low misty light and *hold me close* music, he'd taken Teagan's hand and led her to the dance floor. Resting his cheek against her sweet-smelling hair—one hand holding hers, the other caressing the warm lower scoop of her back—he'd felt as if they were alone, or sure as hell ought to be.

Jacob never made assumptions, but with his senses homed on her body brushing his and her lips near enough to taste, he'd already decided how this evening would end. When he suggested a nightcap, she'd slid her palm down his lapel and curled two fingers into the fabric. Her exact words had been, "Let's do it."

And yet now, out of the elevator and opening the door to his suite, Jacob saw Teagan hesitate, which, of course, made him hesitate, too.

Earlier conversation had revolved around general interests, politics, business. She was into health and fitness, and owned a business in Seattle called High Tea Gym. He'd opened up about the law practice he'd inherited, but hadn't elaborated on his reputation, which was cutthroat. Where litigation against the big guns was concerned, Crush or Be Crushed was the only motto to live by.

When they'd discussed friends, he'd shared a couple of tales about Griff and Ajax Rawson, two of his best friends whom he counted as family and vice versa. He had avoided the subject of blood relations and found it interesting that Teagan had done the same. Not a word.

Now listening to the beads of her gown rustling as she moved into the spacious, lavishly appointed room,

Jacob had to wonder. Everything about her announced poise and class, but there were plenty of ordinary folk who had learned to master the nuances of the privileged, himself included. So was it possible that Teagan's background was similar to his own? Vastly different from all this glitz and best filed away?

Best forgotten?

As she turned, and then smiled again…hell, what did it matter? Closing the distance separating them with a few easy strides, Jacob set questions and doubts aside. What counted now was finally claiming that first kiss. Everything else—including that defamation case against Hunter Publications—would have to wait.

Jacob Stone was so not her type.

As Teagan turned to see him close the door, she reminded herself again, *I like blue eyes.* Lively and ocean-deep. Tender and kind. The preference went as far back as her first crush freshman year.

Mr. Stone's eyes were the kind of focused amber gold that, combined with the jet-black hair, reminded her of a panther—a mesmerizing, muscled male who hadn't eaten in a week. As Jacob slid the key card onto a marble side table and headed over, that hungry gaze locked onto hers and Teagan's jaw almost dropped. He even *moved* like a big cat. Completely captivating, and she was a dog person!

As he drew nearer, Teagan puzzled more. In relationships, she wanted openness and honesty. As much as they had talked this evening, she'd gotten the impression that Jacob was more about control and charm—subtle when need be, direct when the time was right. For instance, she could bet he wouldn't stop his approach until he stood squarely in her space, as close as he'd been on the dance floor earlier. Then, of course, he would offer the same confident smile he had used when he'd suggested a drink here in his suite.

At that moment, with his mouth a hair's breadth away from hers, her body had tingled in all the right places. Caution had melted away. Again, not her usual reaction. True substance, real feelings, including the sizzling sexual kind, needed time to grow, didn't they?

Now, as if he'd read her mind, and just to prove her wrong, Jacob stopped more than an arm's length away. No confident smile, either. Instead his eyebrows knitted while that amber-gold gaze penetrated hers. She felt the tingling again and way more than before.

"Teagan? Are you all right?"

She gathered herself, shrugged it off. "Um, last time I looked—sure."

One side of his mouth tugged higher. "You seem… uncertain."

Tearing her gaze away from his, siphoning in much needed air, she glanced around and made an excuse. "I was just taking this place in."

It was Italian marble everywhere, gold-plated everything, along with perfectly lit artwork that might belong in the Louvre. The excess reminded Teagan of her father's home after his new wife had remodeled. Yes, he was a billionaire but, for Teagan's taste, over the top.

None of the "children" were happy about their dad's second marriage. For starters, stepmom Eloise was more about the almighty dollar than anything else. Nevertheless, they had all supported their father and, of course, their new little brother and baby sister. Family stuck together, no matter their differences—and this clan had a few. But if anyone was in trouble, there was no question, no pause. They closed ranks, now more than ever before.

Jacob was crossing to the suite's phone extension. "I'll order up champagne."

"Actually, I'm good with juice or water."

Without missing a beat, he veered toward the bar's long, gleaming counter. "I'll whip something up."

While eyeing some side shelves, Jacob removed his tie then unfastened the shirt buttons at his throat. Teagan caught a tantalizing glimpse of upper chest. It took her back to their time on the dance floor…to sensations of grazing the hard length of his body and soaking in all that delicious masculine heat.

As he shucked off his jacket, Teagan drifted closer. Beneath the white dress shirt, his chest was strong and chiseled. He folded each sleeve back, revealing two powerful, summer-tanned forearms, then turned to the refrigerator to check out the contents. Teagan told herself not to ogle the lines of his tailored pants then went right ahead and did it anyway.

Long, solid legs.

Even better buns.

Grabbing a stool, Teagan cleared her throat.

"I usually stay clear of alcohol," she said. "The last time I had champagne was at my brother's wedding."

Jacob turned back around and slid a container of chilled berries over the counter toward her. "Nice day?"

"The ceremony was beautiful." It had been a small-ish affair held on the estate grounds in a marquee. "Not quite as glam as this one, of course."

His chuckle was a deep rumble. "Of course."

No need to go into how that day had ended—with

an actual bomb going off. That incident had been the latest in a string of attacks targeting their father. While the authorities were on the case, the madman responsible was still at large.

Nothing you can do about it, so deep breath. Focus on the good stuff.

"I caught up with a friend there," she said, selecting a cold berry. "Our families holidayed together one Christmas. Grace Munroe and I became pen pals, but we lost touch over the years. When I found out she was dating my brother, I almost fell off my chair."

"You mean the brother who got married?"

"Another one," she said, and popped the berry in her mouth.

"So, you have *two* brothers?"

"My parents had four children, me and three older boys. When my father remarried, he had two more—another son and a girl."

"Did your mom remarry, too?"

"She passed away."

Jacob stopped laying drink ingredients on the counter. "I'm sorry."

Teagan nodded. *Thanks. So am I.*

"My friend and brother got engaged Christmas Day," she said, getting back to the main thread while Jacob found two chilled martini glasses. "Funny because when we were young, those two hated each other."

Seeing them together now, those two were so obviously in love—so *meant to be*. Teagan knew Grace and Wynn were destined to grow old together, with gray hair and stooped backs, blissfully content, surrounded by a clutch of grandkids. She was happy for them. Envious, in fact. Commitment, marriage, children...everyone seemed to be doing it. But Teagan couldn't see that kind of scenario in her own future. It simply wasn't in the cards.

Jacob found pineapple juice, vanilla syrup, crushed ice and a shiny silver shaker while Teagan drank in the show. Watching this man move made the nerve endings under her skin quiver and snap alive. And he was just getting started. After tipping in an ounce of syrup, he flipped the shaker into the air and caught it in the same hand—*behind his back*. Not a single drop spilled.

She laughed. "Hey! Good party trick."

"Bartending paid the bills through law school."

Teagan sat straighter. Interesting. He came from money—earlier he had mentioned inheriting a law firm—but he hadn't necessarily relied on it. Maybe Jacob Stone was more her type than she'd thought.

Unlike her older brothers who had accepted jobs with the family company, Teagan had decided to go it alone. The boys had dubbed her The Wild Child, but there was more to her opting out than that. Lately, however, she'd thought about going back. Everyone was on tenterhooks waiting for the next attack. She should be there for her family now.

Jacob was pouring juice into that shaker like a pro.

"Working and studying full-time was a challenge," he said. "But I loved every minute. Passing the New York State Bar was always my dream."

"Do you have a specialty?" Remembering the situation back home in Australia, Teagan leaned closer. "Like criminal law?"

"I deal in reputations. Defamation. Libel."

"Oh, like that case in the news a while back." She recalled the details. "A big-name movie director sued a magazine after they claimed he had indecently assaulted someone."

"The magazine lost." He smacked the juice bottle down like a gavel. "We won."

Get outta here. "That was *your* case?"

"Done and dusted, Your Honor."

Congratulations were in order. But there was a downside. "The amount that director wanted was insane. The magazine worried it would ruin them. That people would lose their jobs."

Jacob studied her before adding a scoop of ice to the shaker. "Not my responsibility."

"Meaning, you'd done your job." *Had brought down the kill.*

"Meaning, if you turn your back on the truth, spread malicious lies, and you come up against me—prepare to pay the price."

Jacob didn't seem agitated. Rather, he looked determined, like Teagan's oldest brother Cole when he was stuck in commander in chief mode. Wynn could be the same way. *Focused,* Grace called it. Even Dex, the chilled middle brother, could switch on that *don't mess with me* trait when need be.

Frankly, the entire family—and their goliath media and news corporation—was known for keeping its eye on the target. Never letting a prize get away. Way too intense for The Wild Child, even if Teagan's father reminded her every chance he got that she shared the same name. That the same blood ran through her veins. He'd said that she couldn't hide from who she was. DNA didn't lie.

While Jacob screwed on the shaker's lid, Teagan joined him behind the bar. "Mind if I try?"

He handed it over. "Be my guest."

She gave the shaker a few slow rotations before going to town. As ice clinked and liquid swished at warp speed, Jacob's eyes widened.

"I'm all about protein shakes, not cocktails." She put a hand on her heart. "I swear."

After she poured the mixture into their glasses, he proposed a fitting toast. "To the truth, the whole truth."

Teagan touched her glass to his. "So help me, God."

She sipped then sighed. Fresh and light and…yeah…

About that toast.

"I need to come clean," she said, setting her glass aside. "I have a confession to make."

"Well, if you need a good lawyer…"

She returned his lopsided grin then admitted, "This is actually a first for me, too…being here with you like this tonight."

His smile changed. The look in his eyes, as well. "As in, two people who just met leaving a party together?"

She nodded. "Needing to be alone for an hour or two."

That amber gaze turned ravenous again. When he stepped closer and a hot palm skimmed beneath the back of her hair—when his head deliberately angled and lowered over hers—it didn't matter that he wasn't what Teagan thought she wanted, needed, maybe even deserved. As his mouth covered hers, there was only one certainty that seemed to shine through. One truth that couldn't be denied.

She was indeed her father's daughter. A Hunter by name. In many respects, a Hunter by nature. And tonight, damn it all, she was hungry, too.

Two

There were times when things felt good. Felt right. There were others when forces conspired or stars aligned and what happened was out of this world.

Like now, Jacob thought, being here with this woman who had come out of nowhere and left zero doubt as to what she was thinking. Where they were heading. Her words alone would have sufficed. The definite yes in her gaze was the icing on the cake.

Let's do it.

As Jacob claimed the first kiss, he felt her dissolve, her two arms coiling around his neck. After blindly setting his glass on the counter, he caressed the curve of her hip while his tongue swept the seam of her lips and they parted. Then she craned up on her toes and pressed her breasts against his ribs. As the kiss deepened and her fingers knotted in his hair, he only grew more certain.

They would need way more than an hour or two.

When Jacob drew away, he kept his gaze on her lips. "Things aren't going too fast?"

A smile played at the corners of her mouth as those gorgeous green eyes drifted open. "Not for me." As she nodded, a waterfall of blond hair cascaded over her shoulder. "How about you? All good?"

So good. Particularly now that she was flicking open every shirt button down to his belt and tracing arcs over his pecs with her nails. Needing to keep up, he found the zipper at her back and eased that baby all the way down. As the gown slipped and rustled into a glittering puddle around her heels, he worked the shirttails from his pants and cast his shirt to the floor. Then he brought her close and claimed her mouth again.

Only now that wasn't nearly enough.

He bent at the knees and caught her around the waist. Then, inch by inch, he lifted her until her silver heels fanned the air a foot above the ground. And that's how he carried her to his bed. Step by step.

Kiss by kiss.

From the minute Jacob had held her on the dance floor—like they'd been the only ones in the room— she had looked forward to this moment. Getting her out of that dress so fast had been a pleasant surprise. When he'd lifted her up against him, his mouth fused to hers the whole time, Teagan wondered just how good this could get.

She was vaguely aware of leaving the light behind… of moving into the bedroom. He adjusted his hold on her waist to throw back the covers. Then, he laid her down on the cool, crisp sheet.

As his lips left hers, she let her arms fall and curl around her head. Siphoning a giddy breath, she took in the sight of him crouched above her. Light filtered through from the main room. In the soft shadows, the strong angles of his jaw and Roman nose looked more pronounced. Those lidded amber eyes seemed to glow. When he smiled, the thrill of anticipation shot straight to her core.

His voice vibrated through to her bones.

"There's something I need to do."

She plucked at the sheet above her head. "You don't need to ask permission."

He came closer. "Are you sure about that?"

She felt a rush of heat. The need to groan. Arching toward him was pure reflex, one that didn't seem to surprise him at all. When he didn't move, she told him again as she bent her knee and brushed her leg against his.

"Yes, Jacob," she said.

Yes, yes, yes.

He eased back, slipped off one heel, then the other, and dropped both her shoes to the floor. When he flicked on a bedside light, the glow was warm and teasing—perfect for taking in his cut torso. But he was still wearing pants while she was pretty much naked. Not a whole lot to hide, including the scar she'd seen reflected in bathroom mirrors half her life. The jagged line was too long and high for an appendix op, and too prominent to go unnoticed for long, particularly given the way Jacob's lidded gaze was devouring her now.

If he frowned and asked—What the hell happened there?—she would tell him straight up. *Fell off my bicycle when I was a kid. Moving on.* But he didn't seem to notice, even when he knelt over her again and his head gradually went lower.

While the tip of his tongue slid along her panty line, one big hand skimmed up her side until his thumb came to rest under her breast. When his mouth slid even lower and he nuzzled her through the patch of white silk, that thumb brushed higher, grazing and flicking and teasing her nipple.

Teagan gripped the sheet, closed her eyes and arched up again.

Sparks were flying, the majority of them having a party under his lips. Then—*dear God!*—he used his teeth. Every pulse point in her body instantly contracted and hummed.

His next words were matter-of-fact.

"This has to go."

Her underwear?

She was ready to rip her panties off herself when he lifted her behind with one hand and eased down the silk with the other. He kissed that part of her before the tip of his tongue delved deeper, tickling and twirling until she was wound up so tight, she could barely think. When he raised her hips higher and slid a finger inside, she gripped his hair as a warning.

Don't stop.

She imagined she felt him smile against her before he eased away, taking that final scrap of clothing with him—down her thighs, past her calves, off her feet. After finding his wallet, he set a foil packet on the bedside table then ditched his shoes and pants while she pressed back into the sheet and took in the show.

He braced his long, rock-solid legs so they were slightly apart. His hips were lean and mean, but it was where the lines converged that drew her gaze like a magnet. As he came forward again, setting one knee on the mattress, one hand on the sheet, she pushed up and met him halfway. Their mouths came together as his free hand curved around her back and she held on for all she was worth.

When his mouth finally left hers, he hummed out a breath then looked into her eyes, smiling.

"You said something earlier."

She grazed her toes up the back of his calf. "You mean about not needing to ask?"

"About needing to be alone for an hour or two." He tasted her lips again and stayed close. "Not long enough."

She traced a fingertip around the shell of his ear. "Are you watching the clock?"

He grinned. "I'm watching *you*." He dropped another lingering kiss at the side of her mouth. "Stay till morning?"

Was he kidding?

Of *course* she would stay.

He rolled on their protection and positioned himself above her. When he pushed inside, she quivered and lost every bit of her breath. In the shadows, he studied her for a long moment before he started moving and slow-kissing her lips.

As he caught her thigh and wrapped her leg around the back of his, she gripped his neck and surrendered it all. And when his thrusts grew faster—when the friction turned white-hot—she squeezed him tighter, bit her lip harder, and came apart like she'd known she would.

Like she never had before.

Three

The smell of fresh coffee woke her.

Blinking open sleepy eyes, Teagan remembered she wasn't in her own room. The bed looked like a tornado had torn through. Shoes and clothes were strewn all over the place. Jacob Stone was gone from the bed, but his musky scent, and the memories, were everywhere.

Burrowing back into the bedclothes, she circled her head with her arms. What an amazing night! The most intense, and beautiful, of her life. From the instant they'd met, those dark, dreamy looks had grabbed her. Accompanying him from the wedding reception to this suite…

Well, it was always going to end this way—with them twined up together, naked in bed. The decision might have been impulsive, but the reality of making love with Jacob Stone had proved to be more than spur of the moment. It was breathtaking, *liberating*, and she would do it all again in a heartbeat.

Grinning, Teagan caught her lower lip between her teeth.

Exactly how long was it before her flight?

Getting to her feet, she picked up on the aroma of pancakes and was suddenly so hungry, needing to refuel. But if Jacob walked through those bedroom doors this minute, she would happily snack on him instead. This was—*he* was—the wake-up call she'd needed.

She'd always prided herself on being strong. Resilient. Then a few months ago she'd suffered a miscarriage, and a relationship she had valued died, too. Now, heading for the attached bath, she felt relief. She could finally look back on that time as a hard lesson learned.

Years after the childhood accident that had left that scar, she'd been told she would likely never conceive. Following her recent loss, however, that prognosis had been modified. Should she become pregnant again, the probability of an early first-trimester spontaneous abortion was high, which had made her feel even *worse*.

But this time spent with Jacob had helped her turn a corner. She would always remember the pain—physical, mental *and* emotional—but she had grieved long enough. She could still live a meaningful and happy life.

Just not the one she would have chosen if she'd had any say.

Jacob heard the shower shut off and waited for Teagan to stroll into the main room. When she did, she was wrapped in an oversize hotel robe, long, damp hair free of salon curls and her beautiful face scrubbed squeaky clean. She took him in, too, in his gray T-shirt and weekend drawstring pants, before studying the room service feast he'd ordered up.

She laughed. "Well, someone's hungry."

His gaze lowered to her mouth. "Always."

They each moved forward until he was close enough to repeat the scene that had gotten things started last night. After sliding a hand around the back of her neck, with great purpose and pleasure, he tasted those sweet lips again.

But this kiss was different. Because it would be one of their last? Or the start of something more? Something new?

He gradually broke the kiss but didn't step away. Being this close again, he felt recharged. Ready for anything, including finding more time to please this woman in every conceivable way.

But first...

"We need coffee." He reached for the silver service pot. "At least I do."

As he poured two cups, she held up a hand. "No sugar for me."

He handed Teagan's cup over then dropped two lumps into his own, as well as an inch of cream. Chugging back a mouthful, he pulled out a seat for her before grabbing a strip of crispy bacon.

Let the feast begin!

After pulling in her chair, Teagan inspected a glass-covered dish. "Is that steak?"

"Filet mignon. Goes great with hollandaise."

There was grilled tomato, smashed avocado, sautéed mushrooms, a pile of golden hash browns and more. It smelled so darn good. But she only reached for the muesli container and shook a modest helping into a bowl. Tacking his smile back on, Jacob helped himself to the smorgasbord. This morning, he could eat enough for two.

Earlier, he'd laid her gown over the back of a couch. She caught sight of it now before eyeing the door to the suite.

"This'll be interesting." She set down the container. "My first walk of shame."

"If anyone can get away with wearing that evening gown this time of day, it's you."

She was busy searching the room-service spread again. *Really* looking this time, like she couldn't find what she wanted. Impossible.

He put his fork down. "Are we missing something?"

"Plant-based milk?"

"Like soy?"

"Or almond."

He got to his feet. "I'll order some up."

Waving him off, she reached for the pancakes. "This is even better."

No trouble, but he wouldn't push. If she was happy, so was he. And after breakfast, before they thought about jetting back to ordinary life, there might be time enough to revisit what they had discovered in each other the night before. Frankly, he wanted to slip the robe off her shoulders, taste every inch of that incredible body, and then do it all over again.

She was looking at his plate. He looked down, too. *Ha.* He'd forgotten all about the food.

As he pushed a loaded fork into his mouth and Teagan poured syrup over a pancake, she said, "I suppose you need to check out soon and get back."

He chewed and swallowed while pouring them juice. "My flight's not till one."

"Mine's around that time, too."

"You need a lift to the airport?"

"No, no. I just don't want to hold you up."

"I'm in no hurry." Watching how she was downing that juice, he asked, "Are you?"

She set down her empty glass. "It's Sunday."

Right. "The weekend. Time to relax. Forget about work."

Although tomorrow would be a day and a half. He had depositions to sort, background notes, too. There was an afternoon meeting scheduled with that defamation client—former Londoner, Grant Howcroft. Hunter Publications was in for a very public kick in the corporate pants. Making up tales might sell magazines but—moral of the story, boys—dishonesty does not pay.

"It must be full-on being a big-name lawyer," Teagan said as she cut into her syrup-soaked pancake.

Was he looking preoccupied?

"It can get busy," he said, loading his fork again.

"Even on weekends?"

Remembering how her legs had dug into the back of his thighs as she'd bucked up against him, Jacob gave her his word. "Not this weekend."

"Are you sure?"

He wanted to laugh. "Absolutely."

"It's just… I've seen that expression before. The *gotta get back to the grind* look."

Sure. "There's an element of that. You'd know, with a business of your own."

"A *small* business. That's more than enough." She

hastened to add, "Of course, people should make their own choices. Ambition isn't necessarily a bad thing."

Ambition was a very *good* thing, particularly when someone had a past like his: a legacy of poverty, despair and *why the hell bother*.

"I had a weird upbringing. Guess that's where I get my drive." He put a little more sugar in his cup and listened to the tinkle of the spoon as he stirred. "How about you?"

"As far as drive goes? I want my business to do well."

"It's important to you?"

"Of course."

He looped back to the heart of the question. "And your upbringing?" Her childhood?

"I wouldn't say it was weird. More filled with challenges, I suppose."

The previous night, they had learned so much about each other, and not all of it purely physical. And yet now, in the morning light, Teagan still seemed largely a mystery.

They both had flights to catch. Nevertheless, he wanted to know more—*feel* more, which was a big step for him. It was the right time, right place.

Certainly right girl.

After she'd finished two pancakes and Jacob had put a decent dent in his generous helping, he dabbed the corners of his mouth with a linen napkin then tapped back into that question.

"So, where did you grow up again?" When they'd met, he'd asked about the accent, which wasn't always noticeable but definitely cute.

"Australia. Sydney." She chose a fat strawberry from the fruit platter. "My family's still there. Well, my father and his wife and their kids. My oldest brother and his wife, too."

"And the rest of the clan?"

"My other brothers are in the States now. Actually, the middle one lives here in LA. He's engaged to someone who grew up in Oklahoma so he spends a lot of downtime there. The other brother's in New York."

"Hey. Small world."

"Wynn's a dyed-in-the-wool workaholic. Although, now that he has Grace in his life, I'm sure that'll change. Or I hope that it does."

In the middle of topping up coffee cups, Jacob hesitated as a chill rippled over his scalp. He shook it off. Found a smile.

"Wynn? That's an unusual name. I'm putting a case together at the moment. The defendant, if it gets that far—" *which it would* "—his name is Wynn."

"Wow. How about that."

He nodded. Smiled again. *Yeah.* "How about that."

Seeming to read his mind, Teagan laughed. "Don't worry. It couldn't be my Wynn. He keeps his cards close to his chest, but a libel suit? He'd have said something about that. Social media would be all over it."

"We haven't submitted yet. No one knows."

Teagan reached for another berry while Jacob finished his second cup of coffee. She hadn't spoken about her family the previous night and hadn't gone into much detail now, not that he'd been particularly forthcoming in that area, either. Admitting that his background was weird was the tip of a Titanic-size iceberg. His childhood had been beyond toxic.

But right now he was more interested in Teagan. And Wynn.

"So what does your brother in New York do? We might know each other."

"How many Wynns have you met again?"

He grinned and conceded. "Only one, and that's on paper."

"So you *couldn't* know my brother."

Ha. Right.

Still…

"What did you say he does for a living?"

Teagan gave him an odd look, like, "maybe drop this." And he would, as soon as this was squared away, because the back of his neck was prickling now. Could be nothing, but he'd learned the hard way to always pay attention to that.

"Wynn works for my father's company," she said. "Or an arm of it. All the boys do."

The prickling grew.

One arm of a family company? "Sounds as if your father runs a big enterprise."

"It's big, all right. Out of college, I decided to do my own thing. I didn't want any part of the drama."

"You're not estranged from your family, though."

Her eyebrows snapped together. "God, no."

"Everyone went to that wedding?"

"Everyone was there."

"So you're all close."

"We've had our differences, between my brothers and father particularly. Too much alike. Although, as they get older, it's not as intense. And, yes. We are close. Protective." She pulled the lapels of her robe together, up around her throat. "That's the way it is with our family. We can say what we want about each other, but anyone throwing shade from the outside needs to brace himself for a smackdown." She set her napkin on the table. "What about you?"

Jacob was still thinking about Wynn and family companies with arms in Sydney, LA and New York.

He tried to focus. "Sorry? What was that?"

"Your family, Jacob. Do you have any siblings? Nieces or nephews?"

"No siblings." As far as blood went, anyway.

"So, it's just your parents and you?"

He rubbed the back of his neck. "It's complicated."

Her laugh was forced. "More complicated than mine?"

Shrugging, he got to his feet. Teagan got to hers, too.

There were questions in her eyes. Doubts about where he'd come from, who he really was. Okay. Let's see.

His A-hole father had jumped ship before Jacob was in school, right before Mom had screwed up monu*freaking*mentally. As a teenager, he'd gone off the rails and literally crashed before lucking out and finding a buoy at just the right moment.

But that was a lifetime ago. So forget about the past and concentrate on this. On now.

Jacob took her hands and stated the glaringly obvious.

"I had a great time last night."

Her expression softened. "Me, too. Really nice."

When he lifted her hand and pressed his lips to her palm, every fiber in his body sat up and took notice.

"You smell so good," he said. Like vanilla.

"It's called soap."

"I skipped the shower. Didn't want to wake you up."

She tilted her head and gave him a teasing look. "I'm awake now."

His gaze roamed her face…the thousand different curves and dips he'd adored and kissed long into the night. Then he considered their backgrounds again, and that *yet to be filed* libel suit. He thought about *his* Wynn, and he thought about *hers*.

It didn't matter. At least, it didn't matter right now.

Leaning in, he circled the tip of her nose with his and murmured, "That robe needs to go."

Her beautiful eyes smiled before she unraveled the bulky tie at her waist. A second later, the robe lay pooled on the floor and they were headed for the bedroom again.

Four

All six shower nozzles were well placed and set to warm and ready. Add two large, soapy hands indulging every part of her body, and Teagan was riding the fast track to *Take Me Now*. Or was that *Take Me Again*? Evidently, Jacob Stone's sole purpose in life was to leave her feeling completely satisfied. Totally adored.

Who was she to complain?

But there were things she wanted for him, too, and precious minutes were flying by. There was no time to lose. So she slid a palm down over that ripped six-pack and curled her fingers around the part of him that so badly wanted to play.

His jaw grazed her temple as he groaned.

"Please say we're not leaving today."

"We have maybe an hour."

When she tightened her hold and slid her hand all

the way down his shaft, he groaned again—deeper this time.

"An hour's not enough."

She grinned. "We're not doing that again."

But when he backed her up to the marble wall and slapped his palms against it high on either side of her head, Teagan seriously wanted to reconsider.

As she continued to work his erection, he lowered his head and tasted a line from the slope of one wet shoulder to her neck. By the time he reached her earlobe, he'd begun to move along with her, falling into the rhythm, his pelvis slowly rocking in time with her stroke. When she'd built up the tempo enough, he gripped her hand and buried his face in her hair.

"Tea… Christ…you're killing me."

"Oh. Sorry."

Not.

"You know I'll get you back."

She whispered in his ear, "You'd better."

Being naked with Jacob Stone set her on fire. As long as their bodies were touching, she felt completely consumed. It was helping to elbow out some of those memories from breakfast.

She didn't care that she was a vegetarian and Jacob loved his meat, or that he wanted to save her from walking out this morning wearing an evening gown. What *hadn't* sat well was their conversation about family.

He'd asked questions, which she'd answered. But he wouldn't let up about Wynn. Yes, it was an unusual name, and she was certain Hunter Enterprises' lawyers had dealt with libel suits before. Sometimes reporters needed to dig around in the dirt to uncover the truth.

Of course, the media should be responsible when

sharing information, but Wynn was the poster boy for ethics—thorough and principled to the point of driving people nuts. Nothing anyone might say, or try to bring against him in a court of law, could ever change her opinion on that.

But now, as Jacob's mouth began working its magic again in a feverous kiss, Teagan pushed all that other stuff from her mind. This slice of time was about filling the well. About being human and truly feeling again.

When his lips left hers, he took his time searching her eyes while she pledged to memory the chiseled angle of his jaw and how water dripped off the tip of his nose. She wanted to remember the way he was looking at her now, like he would do anything to never let her go.

"We wasted too much time sleeping last night." Droplets fell from his black lashes as his gaze burned into hers. "I need to be inside you."

It was a statement of fact. A heartfelt plea.

Yes, I want that, too.

Just one problem.

As compelling as this moment was, safety came first.

Obviously, Jacob agreed. "Condoms are in the bedroom," he said.

"So we should turn off the faucets."

"Or we could go with something else."

She grinned. "Something new?"

"There is nothing new. There's only *better*."

He edged them both around, swapping places while coaxing her to about-face. With his shoulders propped against the wall and that rock-hard body cradling her back and behind, he began nuzzling her neck, caressing her breasts, while one hot palm slid down her front. But when he reached her scar and stopped, she pressed back against him and stiffened.

He kissed the crown of her head. "That's been there a while. Must have hurt."

"I fell off my bike in middle school."

"We should compare battle scars sometime. I've got a couple of whoppers."

As he talked, his hand slipped lower and a finger curved between the apex of her thighs.

Jacob was back to his old tricks, concentrating solely on her. And as he began to tease and gently rub, she forgot about childhood accidents, the fact that time was running out, or anything else that might interfere. She only wanted to concentrate on the outgoing tide and look forward to being carried away.

All too soon, she was trembling and contracting inside. There was a sense of friction building, of everything else blurring and fading away.

His words were warm at the shell of her ear.

"This was a good idea."

"Don't…" She swallowed, caught her breath. "Don't talk."

Pinpricks of heat were flying together, joining and compressing until finally her hips bucked forward, her head rocked back. And before all that intensity came close to burning out, she climaxed again, higher and brighter and, yes, just that bit better. Still touching her, *loving* her, he wrung out the last spasm until she couldn't stand. Couldn't think. She was officially mindless.

Unreservedly his.

But as he scooped her up and carried her to their

bed—curled up in his arms, dripping wet—Teagan knew this wasn't over yet. Jacob Stone wasn't done with her. Not even close.

Nothing was ever perfect, but if Jacob had to come up with something darn close, these hours spent with Teagan would be it. And as much as he had enjoyed the previous night—the talking, the dancing, the mind-blowing sex—this morning's installment in the shower had blown that all clean away.

Now, after making love again, they were lying together, face-to-face, nose to nose. As she looked into his eyes and he looked back, he could only think of the slice of time they had left. Bottom line: he wanted to see her again. But, unless his guess was wrong—and that wasn't likely—this liaison was about to wind up, not for *now,* but for *good.*

The finality of that goodbye hinged on something he needed to say. Something she wouldn't be able to look past. And, frankly, neither would he.

"We need to go," she said, her gaze lingering on his lips. His insides gave a kick that was a whole lot of desire but even more regret.

He exhaled. "How are we going to do that?"

"We get off this bed and say goodbye at the door."

"I don't like that plan."

"Okay. You stay here and I'll pick up my things on the way out."

"That won't work, either."

Her eyes glistened as she smiled. "I think we're out of options."

He came closer and brushed his lips over hers. "Not quite."

Drawing back, she gave him a playful, admonishing look. "We don't have time for another shower."

"No?"

She laughed softly. *"No."*

"Okay. Get ready for Stone's option number two."

He leaned up on an elbow, resting his jaw in his palm as she pushed to her feet and turned to face him.

Waiting, she cocked her head. "I'm listening."

Looking at her awesome nakedness, he was stuck.

"Yeah. I forgot."

Smiling, shaking her head, she headed for the bathroom. "And don't you dare follow me."

He spoke to her through the open doorway. "The walk of shame."

She called back. "What about it?"

"I, for one, would love to see you in that gown again. But we can call one of the boutiques in the lobby and have something in your size sent up. Shoes, too."

Easy. Done.

"That's sweet, but I don't need an Edward Lewis."

Jacob was on his feet, still figuring that out—*Edward who?*—when she returned to the room. She was wearing the T-shirt he'd peeled off before they'd flipped on the shower faucets. It almost came down to her knees.

Striking a *hands on hips* model pose, she asked, "How do I look?"

"Like a goddess."

She blinked and then laughed, but he'd never been more serious in his life. Which made this even harder... what had to be done. They needed to have one more conversation. Better that she found out now, and from him.

While Teagan searched for her shoes, he pulled on his drawstring pants and then rummaged around in his bag for a shirt, which turned out to be a starched business number. Even when he headed off to chill with the Rawsons for a couple of days, he packed one—along with a dark blue jacket and dress pants. That's what lawyers did. Those who ran a firm on Lexington Avenue, at least.

Teagan had slung her heels over her shoulder. She was ready to go. But before she could say another word—*It's been nice...see you next wedding*—Jacob spoke up.

"I'll walk you to your hotel room."

"You don't have to do that."

"I want to." He looked down at himself, his mismatched clothes, his bare feet. "We can do the walk of shame together."

"I'm a big girl. I don't need anyone to hold my hand."

"Then hold *mine*." When she gave a *maybe not* look, he added, "I won't beg. Unless I have to."

She surrendered a smile. "Okay. But remember, we have flights to catch."

He held up one hand and put the other out, horizontal and palm down. "I swear on the Bible. Best behavior."

Her brows pinched and for a moment he thought she was going to say he was trying too hard. Maybe, but not to make an impression or to cling. He liked Teagan, more than any woman he'd known, but he didn't have a stalkerish bone in his body. When he finally said what *needed* to be said, he wanted Teagan to be in the position of power. In her own space. Closing the door in his face if need be.

Moving out of the bedroom, she collected her gown and evening bag while he found the key card. They took the elevator to her floor and made their way down the hall. After she'd swiped and stepped inside, he did it.

He came clean.

"I need to ask you something," he said. "Confirm... something. Your surname. It's Hunter, isn't it?"

Her smile was tight. "Jacob, I told you that last night when we met."

"I, uh, didn't catch it."

"It's okay. All's forgiven."

Rubbing his temple, he muttered, "I wish."

"What was that?"

"I didn't realize it until we spoke over breakfast. About your family. About your brother. Wynn Hunter." *All your cards on the table now, bro.* "He's the Wynn I'm looking to sue."

Teagan's shoulders slumped. Finally, she exhaled. "What a crap note to finish on."

Crap was right. "I'm sorry."

"Sorry that you want to take down my brother? Or sorry that you didn't share this with me before the shower?"

"The last one."

"That's what I figured."

But she appeared calm, as though he'd admitted to liking baseball more than hockey. Where was the name calling? The face slapping? He wanted to sue the pants off her brother, for Pete's sake.

"I thought you'd be more cut up about it," he said.

"Oh?"

Maybe he hadn't been clear. "I intend to decimate Wynn when I get him on the stand."

"I assume that's what clients pay you for."

He dragged a hand down his face, shifted his weight.

"You told me how close your family is. When news of this hits, when your brother receives the verdict…it will affect the entire Hunter conglomerate."

Again. Totally unruffled.

He lowered his voice. "I don't play around in a court-room, Teagan."

"Thanks," she said. "Got it."

Then it hit. Her reaction.

Well, of course.

"You'd already worked it out," he said.

"When you said the case hadn't been filed yet. Before we shared that shower." Her mouth hitched to one side. "I didn't want to spoil things, either."

"So you're not mad?"

"I told you. I grew up with the constant drama of big business. Everything's about control and making sure you're top dog. Kill or be killed." Leaning against the doorjamb, she sighed. "No, I'm not mad. I'm just over it."

So… *Okay, then.*

This didn't have to be goodbye. Of course, they would want to be completely transparent from now on. No more misunderstandings. No holding things back.

He told her, "We won't be able to see each other while I'm working on that case."

"Conflict of interest."

And then some. "But sometime in the future…" Finally giving in to a smile, he edged forward. "We really need to see each other again."

When he moved in to seal it with a kiss, she stepped back.

"I'm afraid that isn't possible," she told him, "and I think you know why."

* * *

Jacob looked like he wanted to laugh, but Teagan wasn't joking. Now that they had reached the crossroads, this was as serious as it got.

"You said you weren't angry," he said. "You said you understood how things work in the corporate world."

"Right. You're trying to bring down my brother. His company. My family's name. I understand perfectly."

"So you *are* mad."

"You have principles. So do I."

Standing in the hall in those smoking sweatpants and an overly starched business shirt, he looked so blindsided—for once, so *not* in control. The moment he'd realized that the man he wanted to suc was her brother, he should have spoken up. But, to be fair, that wouldn't have changed her decision now. She couldn't continue to see someone who was determined to use a courtroom to destroy a member of her family.

However, given the circumstances, she obviously didn't hate the guy. She wanted to show some understanding. Soften the blow.

"I really enjoyed our time together. It was exactly what I needed." More than Jacob, or anyone else, could ever know. "But this is where it ends."

He cocked a brow. "In a hotel hallway?"

"That was your choice." She would have much preferred to have this conversation in private.

"Would you ever have said anything? That you knew?"

"I thought I would if you asked for my number and called."

He ran a hand through his drying hair and scrunched his toes in the carpet. "There's no way around this?"

"Not unless you drop your client. Drop the case."

His jaw tightened. "You know I can't do that."

Sure. "I understand."

Jacob studied her like he was sizing up an opponent. Then he squared his shoulders and summoned a nondescript smile. "I'm glad we did this face-to-face."

"Me, too."

He nodded and then nodded again. "This isn't going to end with a kiss."

"Afraid not." When he nodded a third time, her chest squeezed and she added, "Put yourself in my place. You'd do the exact same thing. Family is family, Jacob. Blood is blood. You can't turn your back on that."

His eyebrows hitched and his gaze dropped to the floor.

"You can if your family sucks."

Teagan blinked. She must have heard wrong.

"Can you say that again?"

"Nothing," he muttered. "Forget it."

"Jacob, did you actually say what I *think* you said?" *That my family sucks?* The idea was too juvenile, too spiteful, to comprehend.

He only exhaled and wrapped it up. "I should go."

Before she could think to pull back, he dropped a quick kiss on her cheek and left, striding back down the hall, disappearing into the elevator. It was all she could do to stop from calling him back to bawl him out.

What a jerk. And to think she'd practically fallen for that guy. Who was one hundred percent *definitely* not her type.

A week later, when Jacob Stone tracked down her business number, Teagan was still fuming. But she'd gotten over her urge to let him know how childish his parting jab at her family had been. She preferred to simply never hear from him again. So she told her receptionist to let Mr. Stone know that she was preparing for an overseas vacation. And a trip was indeed penciled in. So she wasn't lying.

And dealing with the likes of him, so what if she was?

Five

Jacob slammed the phone down, which wasn't like him, or hadn't been in a long while. He'd learned to control his temper, roll with the punches, get his frustrations out in other ways. And, hey, what he'd heard just now wasn't exactly a surprise.

The receptionist at High Tea Gym in Seattle had politely but firmly stated that Teagan was unable to take his call. Ms. Hunter was about to head out of the country and hadn't scheduled a date for her return. She'd be sure to pass any message along.

Translation: *Move on, pal.*

The night he and Teagan had spent together in LA had ended with a massive twist. She was related to the defendant in an upcoming defamation suit. The bigger reveal? They had both been aware of the fact before diving in for an even steamier shower/bedroom finale the next morning.

Jacob swung his high-backed chair toward the window, set his elbows on the armrests and steepled his fingers under his chin as he took in the incredible view of the Chrysler Building. When they'd met, Teagan couldn't have known that a Hunter lawsuit was in his pipeline. She would never have feigned interest purely to gain an advantage…to glean some inside information on her brother's pending case, perhaps. She definitely wouldn't have sex to hold the incident over his head. Nevertheless, a headline had built up in his mind's eye: *Sleazy New York Lawyer Sleeps with Defendant's Sister.*

But, conspiracy theories aside, Teagan refusing to speak with him now was more about *how* they had parted than why. She had said no one should turn her back on family. He'd responded with a dig about doing just that if the family concerned didn't deserve loyalty. He might have used the word "sucked." But he hadn't meant *her* family. He'd been talking about *his*. He was a master at keeping any residual feelings about his background and not being good enough at bay, but at the worst possible moment that old serpent had reared up to bite him in the balls.

The office intercom buzzed. Jacob ignored it. He needed time to cool down, get a grip.

He'd had relationships with women before and, other than one he refused to think about ever again, he'd always been the party to walk away. Everyone got dumped sometime.

Grow up, Stone. It's water under the bridge.

He heard a tap on the door, then his secretary's voice.

"Mr. Howcroft is here," Waverley McCune said in a subdued tone. "He knows he doesn't have an appointment." Her voice lowered to almost a whisper. "He says he's tired of 'all mouth and no trousers,' whatever that means."

Jacob continued to glare at the view, biting his thumbnail now, which he hadn't done since ninth grade, but whatever.

"Jay? What would you like me to tell him?"

Jacob swung his chair around at the same moment Grant Howcroft strode into the room, hands fisted at his sides.

"This bloody well has to stop! I'll see that bastard on his knees before this is through."

Tamping down the air with his hands, Jacob pushed to his feet. "Take a seat, Grant."

The older man threw himself onto a tufted leather couch while Waverley pressed the bridge of her Mr. Magoo eyeglasses back up her nose and quietly closed the door.

"Have you seen social media this morning?"

Jacob moved to the front of his desk, leaned against the edge and folded his arms. "You mean the small-time blogger opinion piece?" Yeah. He'd seen it. The other pieces concerning Howcroft, too.

"I want them shut down." The older man dabbed at his brow with his jacket cuff. "I want them *shut up*!"

"These things take time."

"While my career goes down the bloody toilet?"

"We'll get compensation."

"Tattered reputations don't mend that easily, Jakey boy."

"When the truth comes out they do."

Howcroft scratched at his wiry ginger-gray hair. "According to this latest piece, I'm a sodding drug lord now!"

"It's a piggyback small-time troll."

Grant wasn't listening. "How do I come back at that? I ask you. *How?*"

"By addressing the heart of the lies. By going after the one with the money." Wynn Hunter and his big-time "untouchable" media arm. "We only need to meet the standard for actual malice and prove the accusations are unfounded, which they are."

Then the wrong would be righted and Hunter Publications could kiss both sides of Howcroft's butt.

His client's brow was beaded with sweat. Jacob poured him a glass of water and brought it over.

Howcroft downed half and then closed his eyes at the same time he grit his teeth and his trembling lips turned white.

"I want to see Wynn Hunter destroyed. The rest of his blood-sucking family, too." An image of Teagan flashed into Jacob's mind while Howcroft took another mouthful then eased out a shuddering sigh. "How far away are we from getting this done?"

Jacob went into the fundamentals of where they were with the case. Today was only Thursday, so there wasn't much to add since Monday when they had spoken last. But when a person's life was falling apart, Jacob understood—minutes could feel like years.

Howcroft pushed back into the couch as his eyes darted around the room. "Maybe I should do a runner. Hole up somewhere in Mexico until this thing blows over."

Jacob's chin went down. What happened to wanting to see Wynn Hunter destroyed? "We agreed. This is a process. Now we need to hold our course." Then go for the jugular.

"You know I was born a charwoman's son," Howcroft said, like Jacob didn't research the shit out of his clients' backgrounds. "My first job was as a filing clerk. Respectable, but rubbish pay. I got into theater and climbed the industry ladder from assistant stage manager to walk-on parts. Those first few years were brutal, mate. Young people nowadays don't know the half."

Jacob disagreed. There were lots who did.

"There were a few TV appearances," Howcroft went on, "the move to Hollywood, then the role that launched my career. Instant overnight success, the papers said. There were parties, marriages... And, yes, I made mistakes."

Jacob saw how Howcroft's eyes were edged with moisture and worried he might cry. But his client found his feet and tried to square his hunched shoulders instead.

"I don't know if I can..."

Jacob felt a prickling at the back of his neck. "Know if you can *what*?"

Putting up his hands like he'd heard and said enough, Howcroft headed for the door. "I'll be in touch. One way or another. Probably another."

Which was code for what exactly? "Are you saying you want to put the lawsuit on hold?"

"I'm saying I don't know if I want to continue, period." Howcroft swung open the door. "In fact, drop the whole bloody thing. I need time to get away. Clear my head."

"You want to drop the lawsuit?"

But Howcroft was already gone, which left Jacob wanting to slam the door the same way he had slammed down the phone earlier. He wasn't pissed at his client.

The guy had every right to be upset. If he wanted to put a brake on things, it was his time and his dime.

The thing that stuck in Jacob's craw was the situation with Teagan. If it hadn't been for this lawsuit, their time together would have ended on a very different note. She'd have taken his call today...*if* the time they had spent together had meant more to Teagan than simply letting loose. *If* she hadn't planned to somehow set him up.

After thinking that all through again, Jacob made another call. Not to High Tea Gym this time. To people who had never let him down before and weren't about to now.

The moment the image popped up on her laptop screen, Teagan knew why her eldest brother and his bride were video calling. Good news. The *best.* And when they actually said the words, Teagan promised herself to look happy for them both because she was. Genuinely thrilled.

Attending their wedding last year, hearing their vows and seeing the love they so obviously shared, Teagan had no doubt that Taryn and Cole would last until death do them part. Now, her brother looked proud, but also calm. A huge difference from his former *everything depends on me* demeanor—as if the fate of Hunter Enterprises rested solely on his shoulders. But Taryn's appearance struck Teagan even more. With her long hair draped around her shoulders like a thick, glossy mantle, she looked radiant. Blissfully content.

The couple said it together. "We're pregnant!"

"Ohmigod! Congratulations!" Teagan sucked down a breath and bolstered herself. "When did you find out?"

With an arm around his girl, Cole replied, "Four months ago. Taryn wanted to keep it under wraps for a while."

"I figure I'll be showing soon," Taryn added. "So time to let the cat out of the bag."

The newlyweds looked into each other's eyes like life would always be this way. Bright and wonderful. Never a tear. Although they *had* been grounded enough to delay the announcement.

Teagan could recite the statistics in her sleep: more than eighty percent of miscarriages occurred in the first three months of pregnancy. When fertilized eggs that failed to implant were also factored in, around seventy-five percent of all conceptions didn't go full term.

But this one absolutely would.

Teagan shored up her smile. "So, too early to know if I'm getting a niece or a nephew?"

"We're not sure we want to find out," Cole said.

"We'll be happy no matter what," Taryn added.

"Whichever it turns out to be," Cole said, "we want another one."

Teagan's smile held firm.

More than one. Imagine that.

"How does Dad feel about being a grandfather?" she asked.

Cole's eyebrows pinched. "We haven't told him yet. These past months... It's been tough, particularly recently."

Teagan's heart beat faster. "Has something happened?"

"No more attempts on his life. Unfortunately, no new leads, either." Cole's eyes grew darker. "I don't think he'd care if that madman ever got caught as long as he could stop looking over his shoulder."

"How's Tate?" Teagan missed her youngest brother so much. He was cute and loving, and such a brave little soul.

"We have him over a lot," Taryn said. "The baby, too. It's easier now that Honey's a little older."

Teagan asked, "And Eloise?" His father's young wife.

Cole grunted. "That woman is worse than ever."

Eloise had a problem with the bottle—any bottle she could lay her hands on. She also had a problem with men. She'd come onto their father right after their mother's funeral in her hometown of Atlanta. Eloise had been after a rich man, and Guthrie Hunter was certainly that.

But clearly being the new Mrs. Hunter wasn't enough. Last year, hours before Honey was born, Guthrie learned that Eloise had tried to seduce Cole in the past. He'd been crushed. But, thinking of the children, he'd given her another chance.

After wrapping up the call, Teagan sat back in her office chair, thinking of how happy Taryn must be. But she wouldn't let her thoughts spiral any further down that rabbit hole. She had Tate and Honey, and would be a first-time auntie very soon.

Wasn't that blessing enough?

Pushing out of her chair, Teagan began packing up. She was due an afternoon off. Later she might call some friends. A new restaurant around the corner had rave reviews. Then again, she hadn't had much of an appetite lately…not since those syrup-soaked pancakes the previous Sunday.

A moment later, Teagan said goodbye to the receptionist and left through the gym's main sliding-glass doors. But while she was walking to her car, something caught her eye. A man was climbing out of a cab. Around six-two, killer build, wearing jeans, a casual pale blue button-down and the sexiest pair of shades on the planet.

Teagan's heart hit her throat.

What the hell was Jacob Stone doing there?

He saw her, headed straight over and, in that instant, all the memories came flooding back. Talking, dancing, making love, and suddenly she was tingling all over again, ready to melt.

His clean-shaven jaw tensed as he stopped a short distance from her and removed his sunglasses. "We need to talk."

"So you just dropped in from New York?"

"You wouldn't take my call."

"There's a good reason for that."

"Because of how we said goodbye. I can explain."

Teagan's heart was pounding against her ribs. Her legs felt as weak as cooked noodles.

I can explain.

Seriously?

Continuing on to the parking lot, she gave him the bird then retorted over her shoulder, "And stay away from clichés." *So lame.*

"I grew up with a mother who believed her drug addiction was more important than her only kid," he called after her. "My father was a grifter. He specialized in taking down the elderly and people with special needs."

Teagan pulled up. Slowly turned around. *"What did you say?"*

"He would fix their pipes, mend broken furniture, but he was really casing their homes, making plans to break in and take anything of value. Cash was best, but jewelry, power tools and TVs worked, too. When I was six, he pulled a Houdini. Never heard from him again. His lousy bones could be rotting on Hart Island for all I know."

Teagan could feel her mouth hanging open. Jacob was obviously telling the truth. Who made up stuff like that? And was that a Brooklyn accent she heard coming through?

As he shifted his weight, his amber eyes flashed in the early afternoon sun. "And thinking about it...I *like* clichés. Here's another one." He slipped his hands into his back pockets, cocked his head. "At fourteen, I got into a bad crowd. Smoked, drank. One night, we stole a '69 Chevy Camaro and put the roof down. We skidded out on Pitkin taking a corner. Almost creamed a guy before taking out a pole."

A chill scuttled up Teagan's spine. And her family had thought *she* was wild.

"You were driving?"

"No. Mad Mikey was at the wheel. He turned fifteen the week before and had aspirations of following his brother into the pimp trade. I was riding shotgun. Cost me six months in juvie."

Teagan simply couldn't see it. This refined, powerful, controlled man was once a delinquent? A danger to society?

"Anyway...yeah. That was my life. My family. Who sucked. What I said...it had nothing to do with you. It was all about *me*. I should have told you that then."

"That's why you flew out here today..."

"I needed to apologize." His chin kicked up as his

gaze glinted and narrowed on hers. "And there's something else I need to say. Or want to ask."

Let me guess. "While you're here, you'd like to take me to dinner?" *Followed by a long shower for two, I suppose.*

"I *do* want to ask you to dinner. But home cooked, and not here. In upstate New York. I'd like you to meet my family."

Her jaw dropped again. "Now I'm confused. Your *family*?"

"The people who took me in after the fustercluck that was my childhood. When I needed a real home and someone to care about what I was doing and how I was doing it. The Rawsons saved my life. That's not a cliché or an exaggeration. It's the truth."

She took a moment, let it sink in.

"You want me to fly across the country to have dinner with your adoptive family?"

"Correct."

"You know that sounds *bagful of cats* crazy."

"Yeah. You could say that."

He was forgetting… "Jacob, you're taking my brother to court."

"Not anymore. My client had second thoughts."

"So you're *not* trying to decimate my brother now?"

He grinned and then shrugged. "You'd really like my family."

Maybe she would. They sounded like an amazing bunch. But *come on*. Dinner all the way in New York state? Just like that?

She shook her head. "Not possible."

"You'd be surprised at what's possible if you try."

He started walking toward her again, cutting the distance between them with that languid gait at the same time she remembered the two pink lines on that home pregnancy test a few months ago. She certainly hadn't believed *that* was possible…the most thrilling, completely positive moment of her life.

And suddenly Jacob was standing in front of her and all she could see were those gorgeous amber eyes, willing her to set aside logistics and do this insane thing.

He asked her, "How long will it take to pack?"

"You mean *now*?"

"It's on Friday. The weekend."

But on top of packing, there was informing his family, organizing a flight. She tried to think ahead.

"How many hours does it take to fly to New York anyway?"

"In a private jet—" he reached for her hand "—no time at all."

Six

Soaring eastward from Seattle to New York, the Rawson family's Cirrus SF50 settled into a cruising altitude of forty-thousand feet. Toward the tail end of the aircraft, Teagan sat beside Jacob, wondering what surprises lay ahead. She had flown around the world—finishing school in Switzerland, vacations in the Mediterranean, business jaunts to the UK. Flying across the country should be a breeze, and yet she'd never felt more keyed up about a trip. Choosing to spend the weekend with Jacob's family was pure impulse on both their parts. Come Sunday, would she regret having given in to the urge or would she be looking forward to next time?

Jacob was opening a photo album on his phone. "I hope you like horses. Over the next couple of days, you'll see a few."

"I had some riding lessons when I was young, before—"

When Teagan cut herself off, swallowing those next words, he smiled. "Before what?"

"Before I got into other stuff."

He knew about the fall from her bike and the scar, but he didn't need to know about the consequences. So, enjoying the view—of the man next to her, not the clouds—she focused on the photo he'd brought up on his phone.

"Who's that?"

Jacob angled the screen more her way. "That's Ajax on the back of a prize stallion, Coming Home."

"Wow. All rippling muscle and sleek lines. The horse is nice, too."

Jacob chuckled. "Oh, you and Ajax will get along great."

Perhaps she was being overly optimistic, but Teagan had a feeling she would get along with all the Rawsons. She wanted to hear more about Jacob's adoptive family, the father and two sons who had taken in a troubled teen when he'd needed a soft place to land. And if he wanted to share more about those earlier abusive years, she would listen then, too. Although opening up old wounds could be tough.

Since moving to Seattle, she hadn't told a soul about her accident, the moment that changed her life. She would never forget the pain and how she'd had no energy left to cry. The operations had been endless, and so much time seemed wasted waiting to heal.

But through it all, Teagan had had two parents who had loved her dearly and made certain she was cared for by the best. In comparison, Jacob's childhood sounded like a lonely, desperate, living hell. The memories must be haunting. They must be frightening.

Still, with the Rawsons' help, Jacob had turned his life around. Now he was in the clear, not only surviving but in every way *thriving.*

"Tell me more about the Rawson Stud Farm."

Her hand was resting on the console between their chairs. He took hold of it, grazing his thumb over hers as he replied.

"The property sits between Albany and Lake George, a short drive from one of the country's oldest and most respected racecourses. It offers a full thoroughbred boarding facility along with state-of-the-art breeding needs as well as our own stables. Family owned and run since 1888."

She nodded. "Very informative."

"Like a blurb from Wikipedia, right?" His gaze grew reflective. "The first time I saw those hills and pastures, I couldn't believe it was real. I grew up in East New York. In the '90s, there was a murder every other day. So much robbery and truancy, and don't forget the crack." He shook his head as if to clear it. "I mentioned that stolen car incident. As part of my sentence slash rehabilitation, I was sent to the Rawsons' farm for a couple of weeks. The owner had a program for juvenile offenders. Hux Rawson helped turn more than a few lives around."

"So you went to Rawsons' and never left?"

He gave her a wry grin. "That would've been too easy. After I'd done my time, I got mixed up with a gang that got pinched busting into small businesses—grocers, pawn shops, delis. They took everything they could lay their sticky hands on."

Teagan remembered Jacob's description of his biological father—that he'd been a con man. A thief. "You must've been feeling really messed up at the time."

"I wasn't involved in the robberies. We'd been seen hanging out together, and an eyewitness placed me at the scene of a break-in."

"But if you weren't involved…"

"Over seventy percent of all convictions overturned since DNA evidence was introduced have been based on eyewitness testimony. The human mind doesn't play memories back on cue, like most people think. It reconstructs, trying to put pieces of a puzzle back together. That eyewitness was mistaken, but I went down with the others anyway.

"So I wrote Mr. Rawson, asked if he'd consider having me at the farm again. When I told him I was innocent, he got his brother involved. Uncle Ted, the lawyer, filed some papers, shored up my alibi and my conviction was reversed. But they knew if I went back home, I'd sink into the slime again. A high school freshman with a smack-loving mom and no other support… It's hard to turn things around."

"But you *did* turn it around."

"I will *always* be grateful for my second chance. My second family." Jacob was bringing up another snap on his phone, grinning now. "That's Griff posing with a couple of big-earning mares. He's a kingpin on Wall Street now."

The man was similar in build to Ajax. Both oozed self-confidence and had rugged cowboy good looks. And when Jacob showed her a picture of Hux Rawson, it became obvious where they'd inherited those qualities.

In his sixties, Jacob's adoptive father was still bright-eyed and square-shouldered.

Teagan asked, "And Mrs. Rawson?"

"She passed away before I came on the scene."

That made Teagan feel even closer to the Rawsons. She still missed her own mother so much.

Jacob was swiping again. "Hux says Lanie grew into a spitting image of her mom, in looks as well as temperament. Nowadays, Lanie can be particularly stubborn."

Teagan did a double take. "Lanie?"

"Hux's daughter. Our younger sister."

The picture on his phone showed Jacob, around senior year, with a girl in her early teens. Standing in front of an industrial-size red barn, their arms were looped around each other's waists. Lanie wore bright yellow riding breeches and was looking up at Jacob like he was the bee's knees. Like no one had a brother like hers.

"She's a dressage champion," he said. "Too many medals to count."

Teagan smiled at the adoring expression on Lanie's face. "I can't wait to meet her."

She couldn't wait to meet them all.

After landing at a private airstrip, she and Jacob climbed into a cab waiting in the hangar. As they drove, three thoroughbreds on the other side of a timber-rail fence raced alongside their vehicle right up to the homestead, a cream, shingle-style Victorian that was equal parts grace and warmth.

Huxley Rawson was waiting on the porch. With neat steel-gray hair and a prominent widow's peak, Jacob's adoptive father was indeed tall and broad through the shoulders, like his sons. As they mounted the steps, Teagan noticed a golden retriever by his side.

When Jacob introduced her, Hux ignored the hand she extended. Instead he offered a hug that felt incredibly real. She imagined the troubled youths who, over the years, had found their way here. How at ease and supported they must have felt. How many had wished they could have stayed, too?

"Welcome to our home, Teagan. We're so pleased to have you here." Hux's attention turned to his son and the smile in his burnt-umber eyes shone brighter. "Jay, what a wonderful surprise."

This hug was longer, stronger, with a couple of hearty slaps on the back before pulling away. Without a doubt, Jacob was a good-looking man. But here, in his family home, it was even more pronounced. His eyes were clearer, his voice richer, and the energy behind his smile radiated pure magic, particularly as he turned to study the gentle hills and deepening sunset that had turned the sky into a breathtaking canvas of blue-gray pillows ribboned with rose.

"This place just keeps getting better."

With a hand resting on his son's shoulder, Hux Rawson surveyed the property, too. "If there's a more peaceful place on earth, I'd like to hear about it. Have you been to this part of the country before, Teagan?"

She eased her gaze away from Jacob's profile—that strong Roman nose and proud, jutting jaw. "To New York City," she replied, "but not upstate."

"Jacob mentioned that you live in Seattle."

"For a few years now."

"Is that an English accent?"

"Australian. I get back a couple of times a year. My

father and some siblings live in Sydney." She added, "I'll be an aunt soon. My eldest brother was married last year."

Jacob's eyebrows shot up. "That's great news."

She held her smile. Nodded. "Yes it is."

"Children." The corners of Hux's eyes crinkled as he sighed and angled to rub the golden retriever's head. "Nothing brings a family closer. Your dad must be so proud."

Teagan wouldn't go into details, like how her aging father had a six-year-old and new baby all his own. But, yes, Guthrie would be happy to know he was going to be a grandfather. Hopefully soon he would be able to sit back and enjoy those aspects of his life without worrying that someone wanted him dead.

From the homestead's front doorway, another male voice joined in.

"Well now the party can begin!"

Ajax Rawson's build and gait were bronco busting. His grin was lopsided and the wink he sent Teagan was full of mischief. This was the fun-loving brother who, Teagan guessed, had a hard time fighting off the girls.

The brothers clasped each other's shoulders and shook hands. "This is a turnup for the books," Ajax told Jacob before adding an aside to Teagan. "He works a couple of hours' drive away, but decides to fly thousands of miles just to drop in for a Friday night feed."

Teagan laughed. "Last-minute arrangements."

Ajax gave his brother a playful nudge in the ribs. "You ought to take a gamble more often."

Hux was ushering everyone inside when he stopped to peer off into the distance. Teagan caught the sound then, too—galloping hooves beating the ground, growing louder. Closer. A jet-black horse thundered toward them. The rider was folded forward, yellow breeches raised in the saddle. A stream of dark hair flew behind her like a battle flag.

Lanie Rawson, Teagan thought, charging home to greet her brother, too.

While her horse was still skating to a stop, the young woman jumped off her ride and bolted up the steps, two at a time. Then she hurled herself into Jacob's arms with a force that swung them both around.

Lanie was Teagan's age. In her knee-high riding boots, she was the same height, too. That river of dark hair, with its abundance of natural curl, hung in a wind-beaten braid that ended at the lowest dip of her back. Her energy reminded Teagan of a storm on the cusp, and too bad for anyone who wasn't holding on.

Jacob exclaimed, "What an entrance!" and Hux laughed. Ajax set his hands on either side of his belt buckle as his grin widened. There was so much energy... so much open, honest affection. It made Teagan all the happier for Jacob's situation. She was happy for them all.

But then the picture began to shift.

Lanie peeled herself away from Jacob while Teagan prepared herself for a friendly welcome—perhaps another hug. But the warmth that Lanie had showered upon Jacob seemed to evaporate the instant she laid eyes on her brother's guest. Her wide cornflower-blue gaze hardened. The pointed chin of her heart-shaped face edged higher. Then came her words of welcome, if anyone could call them that.

"So, *you're* what all this fuss is about?"

Teagan had inherited her parents' poise and self-confidence. She didn't normally allow situations to get under her skin. And yet now she felt stuck, wanting to gape. But no one else seemed to notice the goading tone or icy glint in the other woman's gaze. And they didn't comment when Lanie's attention zipped straight back to Jacob and Teagan was left hanging, regrouping...comparing.

This past year, the Hunters had welcomed three women into their family. Teagan had been happy that her brothers had found love, and she was stoked at the idea of having similar-aged "sisters" at long last. On the other hand, Eloise had been her regular hot 'n' cold self, especially when it came to other females. But Teagan had never let her stepmom's selfish personality rattle her. She simply kept memories of her real mother close and tried her best to get along for all their sakes.

Here and now, too, Teagan could have set aside those sinking feelings and concentrated on the pluses. Only one thing stopped her. Something she *couldn't* ignore.

As they went inside to enjoy a cool drink before washing up for dinner, Teagan knew to her bones that Lanie's leveling remark was just the beginning. From the way she held on to Jacob's arm, looking up at him with adoration in her eyes, clearly Lanie not only loved her brother very much, she was protective of him, too. And she viewed Teagan as a threat.

Which was ridiculous. Nonsensical.

Unless there was more to Lanie's feelings for Jacob... emotions that had grown way beyond the scope of an adopted brother and his younger sis.

Seven

Climbing the stairs to their room, which was tucked away in the far end of the stately Victorian's eastern wing, Jacob's thoughts were solely on Teagan. Should he be worried?

When she'd met the family, Teagan had seemed genuinely connected. Happy to be there. But when they'd gone in to talk some more, her tone changed. Teagan wasn't the effusive type. She was composed and in some ways reserved. But there was more to her current mood than that, he was certain.

As Jacob set down their bags, Teagan offered a small smile that he couldn't hope to decipher. If he had to put a caption beneath the expression, it would be: *Landed. Got Here. Next.*

And the way she was looking around the room reminded him of when she'd entered his hotel suite a week ago. Back then, her wariness had quickly thawed. Now? She looked like she wanted to run.

He'd learned his lesson. If something needed airing, sooner was way better than later. *The only approach was total transparency. Nothing but the truth.*

"Tea, is something wrong?"

She'd been studying a filigree-framed mirror hung over a side table. Now her gaze edged across to him.

"Nothing at all."

She wore a casual, flowing, floral dress that fit this rural setting, and her body, to perfection. Although she could never look anything other than poised, her jaw was tight, her pupils tellingly large.

Jacob slid his hands into his front jeans' pockets. "There's definitely something wrong."

"I'm a little tired. Long trip."

"You want to skip dinner?"

"After flying across the country?" She walked over to the other end of the room, which housed two couches, the TV and a bookshelf. "I'm having a second helping, thank you. Possibly even a third."

Looking out the window at the sunset draping the hills, she nodded to herself and then turned to face him.

"Your family is very special, Jacob."

It took a moment to smile. So she *did* like the Rawsons. Well, of course she did. Just for a minute there... But she'd said she was tired. Well, he could promise a relaxing weekend ahead.

"Every time I see Hux, I get that same *now I'm safe* feeling."

Teagan's smile deepened. "I get that feeling, too."

He joined her by the window, close enough for her

to lean in if she wanted. But she only clasped her hands and returned her gaze to the rising moon.

"When was the last time you came to visit?" she asked.

"A couple of months back."

"You'd think it'd been years. They're so happy to see you." She caught his gaze. "Particularly Lanie."

He chuckled. "Over the top, right?"

"A little."

"Believe it or not, when she was young, Lanie was a wallflower with braces, skin problems, next to no meat on her bones. Back then she was waiting to grow into her nose and feet."

"She came out of the awkward stage pretty well."

"Oh, she's *beyond* confident now."

"And beautiful. Mesmerizing, in fact."

"Like watching a comet about to strike."

He laughed while Teagan's lips curved with an overly polite smile. But she must have come across full-on types before. Hell, her own family had a surplus of fireballs. Researching for that lawsuit, he had learned that Wynn Hunter, for example, was an intense character—the kind of person everyone noticed and listened to.

Before flying to Seattle to take that gamble, Jacob had looked into Teagan's family some more. Dex, the middle brother who looked after the movie studio side of Hunter Enterprises in LA, had a playboy reputation, although he was engaged to be married now. The media had painted Cole, the oldest sibling and head of the Australian broadcasting arm, as a domineering hothead, which sounded very much like Guthrie Hunter, the father, back in the day. Recently the Hunter patriarch had retreated from the front lines, handing over the reins to his boys.

There had been some speculation over assassination attempts, too, which had been confirmed when a bomb had exploded at the Hunter family's estate in Sydney during the eldest son's recent wedding.

Jacob had stopped his research there. If Teagan wanted to open up about any of it, that was her choice. Her business. Right now they were discussing his family. Lanie in particular.

Yes indeed, that girl had changed.

"When Lanie was a teen, before I went to college, we would sit together by the main dam and talk about what the future might hold. I wanted to be a kick-ass lawyer, bringing down the bad guys one by one. She only wanted to ride horses and have a family."

Teagan leaned a shoulder against the window frame. "Your sister can certainly ride."

"In a saddle, she's fearless."

"And having a family of her own? Does she have a partner?"

Jacob thought back. Surely there'd been boyfriends, but now he couldn't put his finger on even one.

"I guess she hasn't found the right guy." He grinned as the memories came back. "When she was fifteen, sixteen, she used to joke around and say that one day, if no one else wanted us, we could marry each other."

"Really? And what did you say?"

"I punched her arm and said, 'Gross.' Then she laughed and said it back."

Gross.

"And what about you?"

"What about me?"

"Having a family of your own."

Jacob was caught between wanting to grin and giving her a look that said, *Seriously?* "You mean marriage? Kids?"

Wow. He was coming up with a blank there. Outside of the Rawsons, Jacob's career was his driving force, his focus.

"I've been busy building the firm. I mean, I haven't given it a lot of thought. It's a huge responsibility."

"The biggest."

"I had the worst kinds of role models." He could think of far better things to do than pass those genes on. In fact, he'd rather not have kids. "I don't want to screw anything up."

Like he didn't want to screw up with Teagan again. He had developed feelings for her in a very short span of time. But he wasn't anywhere near ready to think about exchanging vows. And, despite the conversation they were having now, he was sure Teagan wasn't, either.

She had everything going for her, most important, knowing who she was. She might want children of her own one day—he wouldn't be surprised—but she certainly didn't need to chase any guy down an aisle.

Taking her hands in his, he looked into her eyes and smiled. "I'm glad I took the chance and flew to Seattle."

Her gaze softened. "I am, too."

"You look amazing in that dress."

"Who needs an evening gown, right?"

He came near enough for the tips of their noses to touch. Then he slipped one arm around her back and tugged her that bit closer. "I wish there was some music."

"And a dance floor?"

"We could always make our own music."

She cringe-laughed. "Cliché alert!"

"It's not original?" He slowly tasted her lips. "I'm sure I hear violins."

Before his mouth could claim hers, something nudged the back of his knee. He swung around, saw the culprit and pretended to growl.

"Chester? How'd you get in here?"

While the retriever plonked down on his rear end, Jacob checked out the partly opened bedroom door—he must not have closed it properly—while Teagan squatted to the dog's height.

"We didn't get introduced, did we, fella?" When Chester put out his paw for a shake, Teagan turned to marshmallow. "You're not only gorgeous, you're polite."

Jacob hunkered down, too. "He could either be telling us that dinner's on the table or that he wants to camp out here for the night."

"I won't say no."

Teagan was running both hands over Chester's ears and jowls. Chester's expression said, *Love me and I promise to love you back.*

Jacob knew when he was licked.

He pushed to his feet. "While you and Casanova get better acquainted, please excuse me. I'm going to wash up."

He was about to enter the attached bathroom when Teagan called after him.

"Jacob, I really am glad I came."

Good. And when they retired later this evening, he would be locking the door. No interruptions—four-legged or any other type.

* * *

Teagan grew up understanding the power of money. She also knew good taste when she saw it. As she and Jacob entered the Rawsons' large dining room, she was impressed by the nineteenth-century Eastlake chandelier hanging from the vaulted ceiling and the sparkling vintage plates laid out upon a stunning raw-edge maple table.

At the same time Hux and Ajax waved them over to a matching maple wet bar, a set of swing doors on an adjacent wall pushed open and a woman appeared. She wore no makeup or jewelry. Her deep auburn hair was cut so that it swayed like a neat curtain an inch above her shoulders as she walked. Wearing a simple, dark blue linen dress, she exuded a sense of familiarity—or more accurately, a sense of *family*—particularly when she made a beeline for Teagan.

"I'm Susan Copeland." As she smiled, two dimples hijacked her cheeks. "I take care of the house."

"Our Susan does a lot more than that. She takes care of us all," Hux explained.

Susan's smile softened. "And they take care of me."

Teagan didn't miss the look the pair shared, or the way their fingers brushed as they stood side by side. Mrs. Rawson had passed away years ago. Teagan guessed that Susan had come onto the scene sometime after that and had found an ideal haven here, too.

Jacob dropped a kiss on Susan's cheek. "You look beautiful, as always."

Susan smiled at Jacob like a mother should smile at her son, with love and unbridled affection. "For that, you get a second helping of grape pie."

He smacked his lips. "I can smell it baking."

Teagan could, too. The aroma was sweet and delicious. Earlier Jacob had mentioned the district's best-known dessert. She couldn't wait to try it.

"Can I help with anything?" she asked Susan.

"Table's all set." Susan studied the silverware glinting in the chandelier's light. "And Hux just finished carving the roast. So the dishes are ready to be brought out, if you'd like to lend a hand with that."

The men were already in a discussion about a multi-prizewinning mare due to give birth that weekend. As Teagan followed Susan back through the doors to the kitchen, she heard Ajax mention an in-house veterinarian who was examining the expectant mother now.

The kitchen was very large, very clean—all polished, honeyed timber and high-quality stainless steel. And suddenly Teagan felt so hungry. The combined aromas of family dinner at the Rawsons were literally mouth-watering.

"Roast vegetables there," Susan said, crossing to the counter. "Pie's resting, ready to be sliced."

Beyond an expansive window, the rising moon had laced the hills with trails of silver. "What an amazing view," Teagan said, looking out over the land.

"It's a special time of day. So quiet and peaceful, like God himself is getting ready to tuck us all in." Susan joined her by the window. "I'd be happy never to leave this place. What more could a person wish for?"

"I don't think anyone here would *let* you leave."

Susan sighed. "Those boys are like my own. And Huxley is a wonderful father. So patient. Always willing to listen."

"He certainly listened to Jacob when he needed help."

When Susan tucked some hair behind her ear, one

of two diamond earrings was revealed—a sizable yet elegant teardrop stud. A gift from Hux? Lucky woman.

"I remember the day we received that letter from young Jacob," Susan said, "asking if he could come back. Huxley knew the boy was telling the truth, that he wasn't involved in that robbery. And he had faith Jacob could turn his life around."

"Jacob still feels lucky to have you all behind him."

"I know exactly how he feels. When I arrived here, my life was in tatters." She hesitated before opening up more. "I'd been married to a man who treated me like most people wouldn't treat a dog. I stayed because I thought I loved him. Because I thought I could *fix* him. The abuse only got worse. While he was out fishing one day, I packed a single bag and never looked back. When I heard about a job tending house on a quiet estate, I applied and came clean to Huxley about my story. He didn't judge. He never does."

Susan brought herself back from the memory and returned to the expansive center counter. "Have you known Jacob long?"

"We met last weekend."

Rather than look surprised, Susan gave her a bigger smile. "It must have been some weekend."

"It was…" *Incredible. Magical.* "Unexpected."

"Well, although it doesn't need to be said, you are both welcome here anytime, for as long as you'd like to stay. There's nothing better than the sound of family coming together, catching up." As if on cue, laughter seeped through under the doors and Susan sighed. "That has to be the best medicine in the world." She blinked and seemed to catch herself before that easy smile returned. "We'd better get this food out while it's hot."

They each collected a platter. When they rejoined the others, Lanie was there, too. As soon as Teagan laid eyes on Jacob's sister, all the warm feelings from her conversation with Susan iced over. And then she realized... Susan had said the boys were like her own but she hadn't mentioned Hux's daughter.

While Teagan and Susan set down the platters, Lanie didn't once look their way. She was too busy hanging off Jacob's every word, arm looped through his as if she wanted to yank him away. He was simply too wonderful to share.

Hux came straight over to pull out a chair. "Teagan, let's sit you here between Jacob and Lanie."

Lanie broke from her conversation with Jacob to breeze over.

"Dad, I'm sure our guest would like to sit next to you at the head of the table."

Hux looked pleased. "Well, fine by me."

Wearing a white dress with a halter neckline, open back and a billowing ruffled skirt that danced around her ankles—a thousand times different from her breeches and boots earlier—Lanie found her spot on the other side of Jacob while Susan took a chair next to Hux and Ajax.

After Hux said grace and people began serving themselves, Teagan joined in the discussion; they were still talking about the pregnant mare. Ajax was going to check on her as soon as dessert was cleared. Lanie didn't deliver a single word Teagan's way. In fact, she focused her full attention on Jacob.

Then pie was served and Lanie's MO not only changed, it ramped up, like a guillotine blade getting ready to fall.

* * *

This visit was back on track.

Jacob had sensed that something wasn't quite right with Teagan after she'd met his family. She'd seemed reserved. Almost irritated. Then Chester, in all his doggy glory, had wriggled onto the scene and Tea had reclaimed her spark. Over dinner, she'd been her usual self-assured self, enjoying the conversations and fitting in like Jacob had known she would.

Although he had felt a little awkward at times, it had nothing to do with his date for the weekend.

Seated on his other side, Lanie was eager to catch up. These days his adoptive sister was full-on, particularly when they hadn't seen each other for a while. Last time he'd visited, she'd been at the World Cup Dressage finals. So now she had plenty to say. And he really wanted to listen. Except he had a special guest to take care of.

He was neglecting Teagan.

The others were discussing two yearlings going up for sale at Saratoga in August while Lanie was still filling him in on how well her current ride was performing.

"At the start of passage work," she was saying, "you don't want high cadence. You want to confirm the regularity. No uneven steps. Always regularity behind."

"Teagan had riding lessons," he replied, looking at Teagan, wanting to include her.

"Well, we should get you in a saddle while you're here, Teagan," Hux chimed in. "Over the years, Jacob's become quite the master."

"Hux means I haven't fallen off for a while," Jacob clarified.

"I don't have a lot of experience riding," Teagan said, "so maybe nothing too strenuous."

Ajax set down his beer. "Horse riding will give your muscles a good workout. Muscles you never knew you had."

"Teagan owns a gym in Seattle." Jacob added, "She's probably the fittest person here."

Lanie looked around him to study Teagan.

"How long have you owned the gym?" Susan asked, slicing the pie she'd set on the table. "I love Pilates classes."

"A few years now." Teagan leaned in and inhaled. "That smells so good."

"Teagan, you're originally from Australia?" Lanie asked.

Teagan looked around Jacob. "From Sydney. That's right."

"It's supposed to be a pretty little corner of the world." Lanie sighed. "Imagine growing up on an island in the middle of nowhere."

Teagan accepted a dessert plate. "Australia *is* an island. The biggest in the world. Actually, it's almost the size of the States, if you leave out Alaska."

"I didn't know that." Lanie waved away the plate Susan was offering. "I've always wanted to go down and visit."

"There are some amazing beaches and the Great Barrier Reef, of course. The Opera House, the Harbour Bridge—"

"And kangaroos." Lanie fell back in her chair. "They're so funny looking. Like a cross between a cow and a T. rex. They come across as so…"

"Cute?" Susan supplied.

Lanie exhaled. "Docile," she said.

Teagan cocked a brow. "Don't get too close to a big red. You're likely to get your ears boxed in."

"He can try," Lanie replied, slinging a fall of brunette hair over her shoulder. "I don't go down easily."

Jacob's hand tightened around his dessert spoon. His sister had her opinions. She wasn't shy about speaking up—or she wasn't shy *anymore*. But she wasn't normally defensive. So had he imagined that tone in her voice? What did Lanie have to be gripey about? She'd seemed okay a minute ago.

And then...

Well, it got bad.

Teagan and Susan had finished discussing a recipe for a sweet cherry-almond smoothie and Ajax asked for another slab of pie when Lanie leaned forward and set her elbows on the table.

"Your surname," she said while everyone else was scraping their pie plates. "Hunter, isn't it? Dad mentioned it."

"Nice strong name," Hux said, looking at his bowl like he wanted to run a finger around the edge.

"Hunter." Teagan nodded. "That's right."

"Any relation to Guthrie Hunter?"

"He's my father."

Hux paused. "I know that name."

"Of Hunter Enterprises," Lanie supplied. "Broadcasting in Australia, movies in LA. Print media in New York. Very influential. Money coming out of their—"

"Are you sure you don't want some pie, Lanie?" Susan asked.

Lanie smiled. "I'm good. Thanks."

Teagan finished her final mouthful before responding. "I don't have anything to do with that."

Lanie looked taken aback. "You don't have anything to do with your family?"

Jacob spoke up. "Teagan didn't say that."

"I remember catching something on a feed a few months ago," Lanie went on. "A little before Christmas. Is it true?"

Teagan looked calm. Unperturbed. "Is what true?"

"A bomb went off in your father's Sydney mansion."

Hux's head went back and Susan's eyebrows shot up. Even Ajax's gaze snapped up from his plate. "A bomb?"

Lanie was nodding. "I hope no one was hurt."

Jacob found Teagan's hand under the table and squeezed. He wanted to give Lanie the benefit of the doubt. She was curious. But it wasn't so much the topic as the tone.

If Griff and Ajax were his best friends, Lanie was a confidante. Like he'd told Teagan earlier, this brother and sister had a special relationship. But now Lanie needed to back off.

Teagan was responding. "It was a difficult time. Thanks for asking."

"And there was something else," Lanie added, "about death threats against your father..."

Before Jacob could intervene, Susan pushed to her feet and cut in. "I'm going to put the ice cream back in the freezer before it melts."

Jacob was looking at Lanie. What was the deal? It was like she was sixteen again—awkward, overly sensitive. Was there something she needed to get off her chest? Maybe to do with her horses. Maybe to do with a boy. Or should he say *man*? She wasn't a kid anymore, even with her arms folded tight on the table looking like she wanted to break loose.

Like he must've looked fifteen years ago.

Ajax was answering a text he'd just received. "Sorry, guys. I need to head out."

Hux sat straighter. "The mare's foaling?"

Ajax pushed back his chair. "Her water just broke." About to dash out the door, he stopped to study Teagan. Beneath the light, his blue eyes twinkled. "Would you like to see a foal being born?"

Teagan blinked several times before an uncertain smile caught her lips. "The mare won't mind?"

"We'll be quiet."

Ajax wasn't joking.

Jacob took Teagan's hand and was following Hux and Ajax out the door—the foaling stalls were within walking distance—when he remembered Lanie. Glancing back, he narrowed his eyes at her in warning. She had some serious explaining to do.

Ignoring his look, Lanie got to her feet to help Susan clear the table. She had seen her fair share of mares giving birth, but if you hadn't witnessed it before, the experience was something to remember.

But, of course, there were times when something went wrong.

Heading down the porch steps, Ajax's smile was a little strained. "Shake a leg, guys. We don't have much time."

Eight

Teagan hadn't bargained for this. Lanie Rawson's barrage of questions and put-downs at the dinner table was pressure enough. Now she was about to see a mother give birth?

As Jacob took her hand and they followed Hux and Ajax to a large foaling barn, Teagan hoped no one could tell that her stomach was tied up in knots. She shouldn't be so nervous about a natural process. How many births were there every day, every year? But as those barn doors drew closer and she squeezed Jacob's hand harder, Teagan was well aware that things didn't always go according to plan.

Whenever she remembered her miscarriage, every minute played out seamlessly in her mind. More than anything, she remembered the aching sense of loss. Entering the barn now, with the vet quietly waving them over, those memories resurfaced with a vengeance.

She took in the scent of fresh hay and spread of gentle light as they approached a middle stall that was free of clutter—just a clean bed of straw. Her coat shining with sweat, a pregnant mare was plodding around the enclosure, constantly swishing her tail. While Teagan and Jacob sat on a bench that gave a clear view into the stall, Hux and Ajax waited near the railing.

Eventually the mare stopped pacing and lay down.

Sitting forward, Teagan concentrated on the mare's movements—rolling around then sitting up to look at her stomach while Tea continued to hold onto hers.

"She must want this over."

"As long as the foal is in position," Jacob said, "front legs forward, nose in between—it should be relatively fast."

Teagan frowned. "*If* the foal's in position?"

"The vet would have checked."

When Teagan blew out a shaky breath, Jacob put his arm around her and pulled her close. As the mare began to breathe more heavily, she lay flat on her side. When the vet crouched down and shifted her tail, Teagan saw the foal—its front legs, at least—wrapped in an opaque bag, the amniotic sac.

Soon the mare's snorting became more like groans, almost human. Rhythmic, laboring, like she needed this done. The vet was holding—maybe pulling—the foal's front legs while repeating, "Good girl, good girl." But nothing more seemed to be happening.

Finally, there was a rush. The foal's head emerged, followed by the body. Teagan and Jacob got to their feet as the foal's front hooves broke through the sac and its two hind legs were delivered. Teagan could see the new baby's heart beating while the mare lay spent. Happy. Relieved.

She wasn't the only one.

Jacob watched her sleep.

Stroking Teagan's hair, listening to her breathe...this "morning after the night before" was even better than the first time. And not because of the sex. After witnessing the birth of that foal, they had returned to this room, shed their clothes and, aside from cuddling, that was it.

In a week he'd gone from being smitten with Teagan to feeling different...feeling so much more, and to the point of now asking himself a serious question.

Could this really go somewhere?

Could this be it?

She stirred, an unconscious lifting of her chin and rounding of a bare shoulder. As he smiled and waited, her eyelids fluttered, then opened. There was the moment of "Where am I?" before she focused and hit him with a croaky question.

"The foal...?"

"Is doing great. I just got back from speaking with Ajax and Hux."

She pushed hair from her brow and looked toward the window. "What time is it?"

"Time for this."

When his mouth lowered over hers, she hummed in her throat, stretched and then arched in against him, curving a languid arm around his neck.

Of course Jacob had been with women before. Only one had come close to stealing his heart. The end of that relationship had left him feeling like he'd been kicked in the teeth. It had put him off wanting that kind of connection again.

Then he'd gone to that wedding in LA.

When he gradually broke the kiss, Teagan gave him a dreamy *I want you, too* smile.

"Can we see them today?"

Jacob recalibrated his thoughts. She meant the mare and her colt. "You bet. The little guy's walking around. The star on his head's really showing up now."

"Has he got a name?"

"Not yet."

"And when does the father get to meet his boy?"

The question took Jacob by surprise. "Not anytime soon, I'm afraid."

"You mean like in a couple of weeks when he's stronger?"

"A stallion is very much an instinctive, territorial creature. Even when a horse is definitely the father of a foal, sometimes, for whatever reason, he isn't sure."

Teagan looked confused. How could he put this delicately?

"Let's just say that studs don't like competition. It's best not to introduce a stallion to any foal, including their own."

Teagan's expression deepened, and then twisted. "You're saying he might try to hurt his own blood?"

"It can happen. And when it does—when a stallion isn't sure—it's purely about looking after the gene pool. It happens among other species, too. Zebras... well, they're closely related to horses, of course. Some monkeys, bears, bats, lions—"

"Panthers?"

"I'm not sure about that."

It hurt to think about, but there were cases of humans doing it, too.

Hell, maybe that was why the old man hadn't lifted a finger to help him grow up. Jacob remembered Stanley calling him a bastard more than once. Maybe the insults had a more primitive motivation. Maybe he was some other man's biological son.

Just fine by him.

Jacob edged the conversation onto a more pleasant and imminent topic. "I'm going to whip us up some pancakes."

She obviously was ready to drop the subject, too. "Pancakes sound great. Lots of syrup."

"Maybe I should bring breakfast back up here." Leaning in, he brushed his lips over hers. "Including the syrup."

"That might be awkward."

"I won't spill a drop." His lips lingered on hers. "And if I do—"

"I mean your family will think we're up to something."

"Like kissing and stuff? Heaven forbid."

She grinned. "You remind me of Dex."

"Your brother?"

"He likes to think he's funny. And he's a bit of a charmer, too."

"I'll take that as a compliment."

"You *should*. You two would get along." She winced and added, "Or maybe not."

He read between the lines. "Because of the lawsuit against Wynn. That's not happening now, remember?"

"You're sure about that?"

"My client said to drop the whole bloody thing, quote, unquote. No one ever needs to know."

"My family is very well connected, Jacob. My father and brothers have people who keep them informed about all kinds of things, including potential legal threats."

He got that. And perhaps news of Howcroft's shelved defamation case against Hunter Enterprises would leak. Hell, the fighter in him almost prayed that it would. Give them something to worry about other than how to spend their billions.

His tone was dry. "Being part of the elite does have its drawbacks, I suppose."

"Like constantly needing to watch your back."

He hesitated.

"You're talking about physical threats now." The assassination attempts on her father's life.

"Not fun," she concluded. "Particularly for the little ones."

Meaning Teagan's two much younger siblings.

"What your family is going through on that front … I wouldn't wish it on anyone. But my beef with your brother was professional, not personal."

"Somehow I don't think Wynn would see it that way."

He shifted up onto an elbow. "And how do you see it, Tea? Do you really think I'm a greedy predator or someone trying to keep the scales of justice aligned? A person simply believing in and doing their job."

"I think I'd like to see you perform in front of a jury. You're very persuasive." Her lips twitched. "But you already know that."

That was a cue if ever he'd heard one.

He was about to kiss her again, and to hell with

dead lawsuits or pancakes, when his phone beeped. He'd check the message later. But the sound shifted Teagan out of her playful mood. Next time they were alone, he'd turn the damn phone off.

She pulled away. "We aren't going to get side-tracked."

When she got to her feet, his gaze swept over her naked body and he groaned. "That's not helping."

She grabbed a pillow and hid what she could. "Better?"

"It would be better if you came back here."

When he scrambled to grab her, Teagan trotted off toward the bathroom. The pillow might have covered her front, but her bare behind was in full heart-stopping view. Then the door closed and Jacob let out a breath.

He could really use a distraction about now.

He found his phone. A voice mail was waiting. When he recognized the number, he shut his eyes and growled.

What the hell did Ivy Schluter want? Not that he cared. Especially this weekend. Especially *now*. He ought to delete the message without listening.

Except he was a *cross all the Ts* type of guy. He'd listen, *then* he'd delete.

Only the message wasn't anything he could have expected. It might as well have been that a meteor had crash landed at his feet. Or a brick wall was falling on his head.

"We need to meet," the message said. *"It's about us, Jacob. About our child."*

Nine

Jacob scribbled a note for Teagan and left it on the coffee table.

Back soon.
J. XO.

Then he strode out the door knowing exactly where he was headed and whom he needed to see. Not Hux. Yes, his adoptive father would absolutely sit and listen. He always did. Undoubtedly he would offer advice and Jacob knew it would be sound.

But at this stage he only wanted to vent. Get it out. Quite possibly hit something. Ivy leaving a message that referred to "our child" was beyond insane. It had to be the biggest crock ever.

Had to be.

Jacob found Ajax in the stud farm office going over contracts.

"Hey, bro. Your girl ready to pay that new colt a visit?" Ajax put down the papers and sauntered over, a satisfied grin on his face. "She was pretty blown away by it all. I remember the first time I saw a foal come into the world—" Ajax's brow pinched together. "Man, you look *pissed*. Did you two have a fight?"

"No fight. And I don't know what I'm feeling, but anger would have to be up there."

"You want a coffee?"

"Only if it's too early for Scotch."

Ajax was already pouring two cups, setting them up in the sitting area near a set of sliding-glass doors that overlooked the biggest arena. A gray was having trouble settling down—shaking his head, rearing up, hitting back.

"I heard from Ivy this morning."

Ajax's eyes rounded. "Did you tell her to have a nice life and leave you the hell alone?"

"It's more complicated than that."

Ajax finished swallowing a big mouthful of coffee. "Look, no one wants bad karma. Couples split up. It's so much better if there're no hard feelings. No…clinging. But you don't need to play games with that woman. Do not reply. That breakup was utterly—"

He ended with a nasty expletive with which Jacob wholeheartedly agreed.

The breakup. Jacob remembered it well.

First, Ivy's Lhasa apso had come down with a fungal complaint, which, she said, would take up every available speck of her time and emotional energy. A couple of weeks after that, she'd sent a CD with the song that had been playing when they'd first met at a fancy charity do. The handcrafted CD cover read "Let's Press Replay."

There were three months of "getting better all the time" and then, right before a planned vacation to Sweden's archipelagos, because that was Ivy's favorite place in June, she'd sent a friend over to his office to say she was pulling out. When she wouldn't pick up her phone, he'd gone straight to her apartment. She'd spoken to him via the intercom. The general gist was, "Why arc you bothering me? Goodbye for good." He'd punched the panel a couple of times before getting himself together. There had been no further contact until now. Until this.

Jacob put his head in his hands and took a few deep breaths. He felt his brother's hand patting and rubbing his back.

"It's really shaken you up."

"Jax, apparently I'm a father."

His brother frowned and then blinked. When comprehension finally hit, he jolted and slopped coffee all over the place.

"A father? Since when? You guys broke up a freaking year ago."

"The baby would have to be three or four months old. Or more."

"How do you feel about it? Other than being livid knowing that she should have told you way sooner than this."

"I feel… I don't know. Numb? Surreal?" Jacob cupped his hands around his mouth and breathed in and out. He'd never had a panic attack but now seemed the perfect time to start.

"I can't believe it, you know. We always used protection. I understand that nothing is one hundred percent safe…"

"Have you stopped to think that it might not be yours?"

"Of course I have. Then I thought, why the hell would anybody do that? Even Ivy."

Ajax's shoulders squared. "Straight off the bat, you need to have that checked out, not only for your sake but for the child's."

"Absolutely."

And if he *was* this baby's daddy, of course he would step up. If he wasn't… He'd have dodged a mighty big bullet. He pitied anyone who had to coparent with someone like Ivy Schluter.

But right now…

"How do I tell Teagan?"

Ajax's grin was lopsided. "You like her a lot."

"A *lot* a lot."

"Hold back. Ivy could be playing another one of her games." He pulled a face like he'd sucked a rotten grapefruit. "That woman is so superficial. I have no problem with people coming from money, but it grates when they need to let everyone know. I'm pretty sure Ivy's the type to have her own professional picture hanger and kidnap insurance." Ajax put his boots up on the end of the table and threaded his fingers behind his head, his favorite thinking posture. "She never asked you to meet her folks, did she? We all met *her*."

"It didn't seem like a big deal at the time."

"If a girl doesn't want you to meet her family, she's not serious." Ajax's lip curled. "Ivy was *never* serious."

"She was serious enough to have my child."

Ajax grunted. *We'll see.* "So, a boy or a girl?"

"She didn't say. Doesn't matter. He or she will need my support."

"Money and the other kind. The most *important* kind."

Acceptance and buckets of love. Given his own history, Jacob was determined to let this child know he was anything but a burden.

If this child is mine.

Ajax circled back to Jacob's question. "So, breaking the news to Teagan…" He wrinkled his hawkish nose. "Seriously, don't say anything yet."

"I can't act like nothing's happened." Jacob told Ajax about the mix-up when he and Teagan had both guessed that the man he had wanted to take to court and her brother were the same.

Jacob nodded. "It's going to be hard." *Maybe even fatal.* "But I won't hold anything back from her. Not again."

Teagan had finished showering and was reading Jacob's note when her phone pinged. It was a message from Grace Munroe. Apparently, Grace *Hunter* as of this week.

Tea, your wonderful brother and I have tied the knot! We both agreed that small was better. No stress and more time for the honeymoon. Which brings me to… We're visiting your family on our way back from Italy. (Doesn't Venice sound like the ideal honeymoon escape?) If you could make it, Wynn and I would love to see you in Sydney. Will video call as soon as we have more deets. XOXO

The friends hadn't seen each other since Taryn and Cole's wedding last year. The start of that day had been as magical as the end—the explosion—had been horrific. Then stepmom Eloise had gone into labor. Around the same time, Guthrie had learned that his young wife had put the moves on his oldest son.

There was just no way to get your head around that.

In the new year, back in Seattle, Teagan had gone through her own crisis—the miscarriage. Although she was the one to end the relationship, once Damon Barringer had discovered her reason, he hadn't put up a fight.

Now, months later, she was seeing someone new. A man her family would happily shun once the truth about that lawsuit came out. Jacob's ability to argue a point wouldn't make a scrap of difference where Wynn was concerned. Not that she had ever considered introducing them. The thought had never entered her head. Or not seriously.

Until now.

Setting aside Grace's invitation and the phone, Teagan slipped into a pair of three-quarter-length pants, a sleeveless shirt and gym shoes. While she ran a brush through her hair, she wondered more. Her relationship with Jacob certainly hadn't traveled a conventional route. She'd been ready to say goodbye after their night, and morning, together in LA. But that misunderstanding surrounding his "family sucks" comment had been cleared up. And now she couldn't deny she wasn't unhappy that Jacob had pursued her. He'd pulled out all the stops to make this weekend happen, and she had enjoyed meeting his family...minus Lanie, of course. The chemistry she and Jacob shared was something she had never experienced before, even with Damon, a man she had adored.

She hadn't invited Damon to Cole and Taryn's wedding; she hadn't been able to see a future for them together. Damon came from a big family, and one of his biggest priorities was having one of his own. After her home pregnancy test, there'd been a brief window of time when she had begun to believe it was possible. But after the miscarriage, when doctors had confirmed any subsequent (unlikely) pregnancies would fail in the first trimester, she and Damon had talked. They'd touched on the surrogacy option. He wasn't convinced; too many risks and complications. When adoption was brought up, despite the brave face, he had obviously wanted more.

Teagan didn't know how Jacob felt about being a parent. Frankly, this minute, she didn't want to think about it. Wasn't it enough to simply enjoy this time they had together?

Her brothers were all settled with lifelong partners. She would like to have someone special at her side this coming family visit, too. And as dangerous as it might sound, regardless of the risks, she would love for that someone to be Jacob.

When she turned and saw the unmade bed, her insides fluttered with longing. She and Jacob hadn't made love the previous night. After watching the birth of that foal, she'd preferred to simply curl up and soak in his heat before dropping off to sleep. But she was looking forward to being alone with him tonight. Heck, she was looking forward to seeing Jacob walk back through that door.

On cue, the door fanned open and Teagan felt the *zap*. Tall and built, Jacob looked so sexy in jeans and a button-down shirt, especially with that wedge of throat and chest visible at his open collar. With morning light slicing in through the window, his amber eyes were narrowed and even more intense.

He crossed over to her and, without a word, clasped her shoulders and drew her in for a kiss that reduced her to a steamy mess. Apparently he'd missed her, too.

When he broke the kiss, she gripped his shirt and pulled him close again.

"Where'd you go?"

"To see Ajax."

"Oh, yeah. How come?"

Jacob's gaze followed his hand as he pushed hair away from her cheek. "I was probably gone too long."

"You weren't gone too long." She fanned her palms over the hard, hot expanse of his chest. "But I'm happy you're back."

"I'm happy you're happy."

Something different in his eyes made her stop and look deeper. What had he and Ajax discussed? Family stuff, no doubt. His business, not hers. But she did have some news of her own to share.

"A text came in while you were out. Wynn and Grace got married on the quiet. They're visiting Sydney soon to celebrate with family. They asked if I could fly out."

He nodded. Shrugged. "Of course."

Teagan paused. Was it imagination or was he acting low-key weird, like he wasn't certain what to say or where to look? Did the mention of Wynn make him feel awkward? It shouldn't. Earlier he'd said that his conflict with her brother was professional, not personal.

She took a step back. "It'll probably be in a couple

of weeks. I'm really looking forward to seeing everyone again."

"Right." His eyes glazed over. "Family is important. Is everything."

A chill raced up Teagan's spine. What the hell had happened since he'd left her earlier? He'd seen Ajax. Had he spoken to Lanie, too?

Teagan crossed her arms. She had wondered about inviting him to Australia. Now she wanted to put it out there just to get his reaction.

"Would you like to join me?"

He blinked and then frowned. "Join you where?"

"In Sydney. You could meet everyone. They could meet you."

When he only looked at her—or rather *through* her—she felt that chill again.

She held his arm. "For God's sake, Jacob, what's wrong?"

He shut his eyes tight, rubbed his brow. "I received a message this morning, too. It was from my ex. Ivy and I broke up a year ago. I almost deleted the message sight unseen. But she had something to share...about family."

"Is someone ill?" He shook his head. "Passed away?"

"There's been a birth."

"So...congratulations."

"That's pretty much how she ended the message."

"I don't understand."

But the strain bracing his jaw, the stormy depth in his gaze...

Suddenly all the blood fell from Teagan's head to the soles of her feet.

Jacob and this woman had broken up a year ago,

there'd been a birth, and the ex was passing on her congratulations...

"Your ex had a baby?"

"Apparently so."

"*Your* baby, Jacob?"

"That's what she said."

Teagan waited for the buzzing in her brain to subside. Then, feeling unsteady, she took a seat on the edge of the mattress. *That's what she said.*

Teagan pinned him with a look. "You think she's lying?"

"I didn't say that."

"Have you called her?"

"I'll wait till Monday."

What the...? "You can't wait that long."

He was pacing to the window and back again. "Crazy, but I'd have liked a little more time to prepare."

At the risk of sounding entirely selfish, so did *she*.

Her chest felt so tight. The backs of her eyes were burning. She had taken a chance and accepted an invitation to spend the weekend with a man she barely knew. It turned out she knew far less than she could ever have imagined.

She got to her feet, got a grip. The situation called for civility, but she deserved some answers.

"Why did you break up?"

"I think she got bored. I was cut up about it at the time. But Ivy and I were never going to make it. She comes from big money. A *huge* sense of entitlement."

Teagan bristled. "Wealth doesn't *always* mean a sense of entitlement." Case in point.

Jacob was so preoccupied, her last remark didn't seem to register.

"I spoke to Ajax about it," he said. "We couldn't work out why she hadn't contacted me sooner."

"Maybe she was afraid. Maybe she'd only just worked up the courage to tell you."

"I don't think Ivy's afraid of anything."

Okay. "Maybe she wanted to bring the child up herself."

"Why? I'm not some *creep.* If he's mine, of course I'm gonna look after him."

Teagan paused. There was that Brooklyn accent again.

He was pacing again, talking to himself more than to her. "Obviously, I need to make sure the baby is mine."

"Would this woman lie about something like that?"

"She could've gotten the dates mixed up. In which case, not my baby. Not my problem."

Teagan flinched.

Jacob's world had been flipped on its head. He needed time, and he needed it without distractions. And, from her end, she needed to get out of there—the sooner, the better.

"Jacob, we need to cut this weekend short."

He shot a glance at her like he wanted to disagree. But then his shoulders drooped and he walked to the window again. Finally, he nodded.

"Bad timing."

As upset as she was, Teagan wanted to comfort him. But her thoughts were suddenly so crowded. She was thinking about little Tate and Honey, and her miscarriage, as well as Ivy's new baby. And she was thinking about that foal's father, too—a powerful, instinctive male who couldn't necessarily be trusted to bond with his own spawn.

Ten

Taking a seat behind her office desk, Teagan patted her postworkout face with a towel as she brought up emails.

Ah. A confirmation from the travel agent. And Grace had sent word that she and Wynn had landed in Australia. Her own flight was due to depart Sea-Tac later that evening. *Home, sweet home, here I come.*

She couldn't wait to raise a glass to the newlyweds. The second toast she had planned would be just as thrilling—to Cole and Taryn on their baby news. She needed to see and hug her dad again. She was desperate for a cuddle from her darling Tate, and her heart ached to hold little Honey. The latest addition to the Hunter clan was six months old now.

Not much older than Jacob Stone's child.

If the baby was indeed his.

After cutting short their weekend at the Rawsons',

Jacob had phoned from New York. They'd reminisced over details of their trip, particularly the birth of the foal. Then he'd apologized again for "screwing it up." He'd gone on to say that he'd set up a meeting with the ex to ask some initial questions. In closing, he'd said how much he missed Teagan...that he couldn't wait to see her. He had promised to phone again soon.

Jacob's second call had been brief. The meeting with the ex had been delayed. Prickly Ivy was trying his patience. He'd sounded on edge.

That was three weeks ago.

Closing her eyes, Teagan sat back and drew her palm across the raised scar beneath her sweat-damp top. There were so many questions.

Was Jacob the father of Ivy Schluter's baby? Given the lapse between phone calls, Teagan guessed probably yes. Would Jacob marry Ivy for the baby's sake? Perhaps, if he thought that would give his child the stable home life he had never enjoyed growing up.

If Jacob called again, how would she react? Hopefully with grace, although she had fantasized about hanging up in his ear. He'd left her hanging. Just plain rude.

And then there was the most obscure and haunting question...the one that spoke directly to her miscarriage and she couldn't seem to drown out.

Had Ivy been pregnant before? Had she ever lost a baby?

These last few months Teagan had pored over stories of others who had suffered similar losses to her own. Even after multiple miscarriages, which weren't at all uncommon, many rallied to try and try again. Teagan had nothing but respect for those women and their partners. She could never face that kind of heartache twice, let alone a third, fourth or fifth time.

Hitting Print on the email containing her flight information, she thought of Jacob again. Their short time together had been amazing, but now she hoped he wouldn't try to contact her again. She didn't need apologies and the *thanks for being so understanding* treatment. She only wanted to be left alone to concentrate on her own life and what she *did* have, which included a growing family...just not a family of her own.

The restaurant accepted bookings three weeks in advance, which was why she had needed to postpone their meeting. The new chef was the crème de la crème, Ivy had said. The patrons here of a similar ilk.

Oh, puh-leeze.

Now as the maître d' ushered Jacob to a booth, he made an effort to push all that crap from his mind. But he couldn't block out the name Ivy had chosen for her boy. Benson Rockwell. Sounded like a character from a vomit-inducing rom-com. And that was the last time he would think that way. This kid needed to know that everything about him was amazing, including his handle. He could totally work with Benson... Ben, Benny.

How about Buddy?

Now *that* was a cool name.

As Jacob neared the table, Ivy saw him and sat up, preening in her white silk blouse. She was as beautiful as he remembered, although the copper-colored hair wasn't quiet as styled and her makeup lacked her former meticulous technique. But being a new mother would mean cutting back on "Ivy time," even with a nanny and laundry service. Jacob imagined her parents would help out, too, which he appreciated.

He guessed he'd finally get to meet the family.

As he drew closer, Jacob dragged his damp palms down the sides of his pants. There was no baby stroller around, and Ivy wasn't holding a baby, either. Perhaps Buddy was lying or sitting on the cushioned seat beside her. Then Jacob got closer.

*Un*freaking*believable.*

Jaw clenched tight, Jacob rubbed the back of his neck. "You didn't bring him, did you?"

Ivy's spider-leg lashes grew heavy. *Bor-ring.* "This isn't your local pizzeria, Jacob."

Jacob felt his lip curl. He should tell her that *he* would choose the venue next time. Walking out would feel even better. But that baby deserved at least one rational parent.

So he took a seat, cleared his throat. With fingers locked together on the tabletop, he proceeded in a calm and mature manner.

"Ivy. We agreed. You said you would bring him."

Looking innocent—or trying to—she swirled her creamy mocktail. That was one thing he could rest easy about. Ivy had her faults, but she wasn't a lush. And she would never do drugs.

"I thought we could talk more easily without having to soothe him every five minutes."

Jacob frowned. "He needs a lot of soothing?"

She brought the straw to her painted lips. "No more than other babies, I suppose."

"Do you have any photos?"

He had held off asking. It made no sense to drive himself crazy comparing noses and eyes, searching for signs that junior looked like his old man. And he'd had *every* intention of having a paternity test performed by now. Why get emotionally invested, analyze baby pictures, if the point was moot? But days and weeks of no contact had crawled by. Now, damn it, he needed a visual.

Setting the glass aside, Ivy dawdled, finally finding her phone. While Jacob clasped his hands tighter, he watched the inch-long acrylic nail tip swipe, and swipe, and swipe again. Finally, she handed the device over.

The album contained shots of a newborn with mom at the hospital, one in a car capsule, another being held by a woman who looked besotted and a little worn.

"Who's that?"

Ivy glanced at the screen. "Mother. *Granma*."

Jacob looked harder. Holy crap. She was kidding, right? But there wasn't a hint of humor in Ivy's icy-green gaze.

"Mom knows practically everything about diaper rash and colic."

"He has colic?" Wasn't that when a baby cried and hurled all the time?

"He's over it now." Ivy shuddered. "Never going through *that* again."

And the woman—Granma—that *couldn't* be Ivy's mother. Where was the privileged air and haute-couture outfit? She looked like someone's eccentric great-aunt. But one should never judge a book by its cover. And if Ivy's mother was…well, *reserved* in her desire to appear privileged, it kind of made sense that her daughter might rebel and flaunt it every chance she got.

Ivy was tapping that fake fingernail on the table like,

Enough with the small talk already. "We need to discuss child support."

He handed the phone back. "And visitation."

"Thoughts?"

"I'd like every other weekend."

She looked severely underwhelmed.

"And we need to organize that paternity test," he told her again, like he had during all their phone conversations. "They're accurate. Ninety-nine point nine-nine percent on a positive match. Zero if it's negative."

"Well, he's got your eyes."

Jacob snatched back the phone. "He does?"

"They were blue at first but going brownish now."

Brownish? Teagan said his eyes were amber-gold. She said she'd never met anyone with eyes like his.

He couldn't count the times he'd debated calling Teagan these past weeks. He remembered how his body had reacted whenever they'd made love…how good it had felt to simply watch her sleep. He wanted to move forward with the relationship, but that couldn't happen until *this* situation was sorted. When he spoke to Teagan next, he wanted to have all the answers as well as a plan.

And the first step, damn it, was that *test*.

"I've been in touch with a reputable professional," he said while Ivy collected her menu and scanned the appetizers. "The sooner we get that out of the way, the better. Don't you agree?"

"Uh-huh." She turned the page. "The sooner, the better."

His temples began to throb. Steam was rising from around his collar.

"For God's sake, Ivy, this isn't a game."

"Of course it's not a game." She slapped down the

menu. "That's insulting, Jacob. It's insulting to *Benson*. If you don't want to take care of your own son, just tell me now."

His gut twisted so sharply, he groaned. "I would never try to run away from my responsibility." Never in a million years.

Looking into his eyes, she slanted her head, exhaled and then reached for his hand. When her fingers curled around it and her nails dug in, he wanted to pull away. He didn't need this contact. With or without a baby, that boat had sailed long ago.

He hoped that his expression said it all.

We're a team in this, but not "together."

Then he slid his hand from beneath hers.

Sitting back, Ivy returned her attention to the menu. She tapped on an item. "I need to try the duck liver crème brûlée," she said. "Definitely the hazelnut soufflé for dessert."

Eleven

"Sorry I didn't call sooner."

Teagan wanted to laugh. As if those words were in any way near good enough.

"I guess you've been busy," she replied, gazing, unseeing, from the back seat of a cab on her way from Sydney Airport to her father's house.

"I didn't want to phone until there'd been some movement," he said. "I just got back from giving a sample for a paternity test."

Teagan's stomach muscles twisted. She'd been making headway getting over Jacob Stone, pushing him plum out of her mind. What had begun with a bang had run out of gas and ultimately died. As far as his paternity test was concerned? *Good luck.*

And goodbye.

"Teagan?"

She didn't want to talk. She wanted to hang up then calmly pitch her phone out the window so he couldn't call again.

His voice in her ear was low and rich.

"Tea, I don't blame you for being angry."

"I am not *angry*."

She wouldn't allow herself to be. She was simply a tad busy herself now. After her flight had touched down ahead of time, she had called Wynn to say to expect her soon. Her brother had said he'd be there in thirty minutes to collect her. But as she had told Jacob, she was a big girl. She could deal on her own, and had hailed a cab.

"Ivy's being Ivy," Jacob was saying.

Sorry. Not interested. But she let him get it all out—the story behind finally meeting with the ex and how she hadn't brought the baby along as agreed. He'd seen photos, though. It was a boy. Benson. Lovely name. Not that Teagan's opinion mattered one bit.

And as the rehash went on, Teagan's grip on the phone tightened. This conversation brought back memories she didn't need now…the excitement of seeing those pink lines form on the stick from the home pregnancy kit…the bliss of anticipating sonogram images, hearing first words, seeing first steps.

Jacob had come full circle. He was back on the paternity test now.

"The results will take anywhere from a few days to three weeks."

The cab was nearing her street. She wanted to be focused—*happy*—when she saw everyone again.

"Teagan? Are you there?"

"Uh-huh. Needing to cut this short, though."

And then the cab pulled into the driveway and, in the distance, the Hunter mansion came into view, a huge, white structure set in an idyllic leafy enclave. The understanding hit her like a medicine ball to the gut.

God, I'm glad to be home.

"I'll call later," Jacob said.

As a security man opened the electronic gates, Teagan swallowed against the ache that had grown to the size of a peach in her throat. "I'm tied up for a week or two. So…good luck with it all."

He hesitated before grunting.

"Wow."

She frowned. *"Wow* what?"

"Nothing."

She pulled the phone away from her ear. Time to hang up. But then she caught his next words.

"Tea, a bomb exploded in my life and I'm still sorting through the pieces."

The cab was rolling down the drive, past the area where last year's wedding marquee had stood…the place where the blast had gone off and precious lives had almost been lost.

"I know I left you hanging," he went on.

She pressed her lips together as tears stung behind her eyes.

"I need to go."

"We can't do this over the phone," he said. "We need to talk face-to-face."

She was gripping the door handle, needing to get out. "Not possible."

"I'll fly over."

He thought she was in Seattle. "You'd need to add another twenty thousand miles to the trip. I'm in Australia." Before he could interrupt, she wrapped it up. "We had a nice time." The absolute best of her life. "But it was two nights followed by two phone calls. We don't owe each other anything."

As the cab approached the front doors, she heard him exhale.

"How long are you out of the country?"

"A week. Maybe longer." She closed her stinging eyes. Why was she even telling him this?

"I'm coming over," he said.

She coughed out a laugh. "No, you are not."

"I should have called sooner."

"You already said that."

"You wanted me to meet your family."

"That was before—"

"Before I was a plus one?"

Did he mean the baby?

She withered, shook her head and murmured, "That's not it."

"Tea, I want to see you. I need to *hold* you. A few hours on a plane…"

She didn't respond. That ache in her throat was so big now, she didn't know whether she could.

He asked her, "Did I read us wrong?"

"You weren't reading anything wrong three weeks ago," she told him as the cab pulled up. "We don't have anything more to say."

Long pause, then…

"Okay."

She breathed out. *Finally.* "Okay."

"You have a great time with everyone."

She would. And she was going to hang up.

Damn it, she wasn't being a bitch.

Still, she had to add, "This isn't going anywhere."

"Okay."

"Anyway... I can't just tell everyone that you're coming over out of the blue. They have no idea I was seeing someone."

"Okay."

"Stop *saying* that," she snapped.

"Okay." When she growled again, he chuckled. Then, "No. Really. I understand."

She held her roiling stomach and closed her eyes. "No, you don't understand." There was so much he *didn't* know. Would *never* know.

"If you're happy, I'm happy for you."

"That's a cliché." But she almost grinned as she said it.

There was another long pause before he admitted, "I wish I could hold you right now."

"Well, you can't."

The driver was taking luggage from the trunk. Soon she would be inside, hugging her family, not listening to Jacob's deep, rumbly, gorgeous voice that made her remember the amazing color of his eyes and the incredible way he made her feel when they touched... when they kissed.

She bit her lip but the tingling only grew.

"Jacob?"

"Yeah?"

Damn it. "I miss you, too."

"I'll be there in twenty-four hours. Okay?"

She eased out a smile and nodded. "Okay."

And then she saw Grace hurrying out through the front doors, waving her arms, pointing to a sparkling diamond solitaire and gold band on her wedding finger.

While her friend did a fairy-tale twirl, Wynn appeared and the driver opened Teagan's door. She told Jacob, "I have to go," and as she approached the steps, her brother strode forward with a *just married* grin plastered across his face. Wynn grabbed her up, swung her around and Teagan finally cast Jacob Stone from her mind.

Of course, that didn't last long.

July in Australia was the middle of winter. In Sydney, temperatures were traditionally mild. Early frost and fog were common. In all recorded history, the sands of Bondi Beach had been covered in snow only once. On the morning of June 28, 1836, the colonial outpost had awoken to a drift that coated the streets in a crisp white fall an inch deep.

Today, however, was all endless blue skies and seventy-five degrees—more than comfortable enough for a mug of something warm while lounging outside on the patio area near the pool. As Teagan and Grace strolled out holding hands, with Wynn a step behind, the rest of the family turned in their seats.

Cole sent over a salute before bringing his beautiful wife close. Resting a gentle hand on her belly, he mouthed the words, *Baby on board.*

So much taller—and older—than he'd looked a few months earlier, Tate sprinted over. He didn't stop until he flew into her arms. Swinging him up, she held on tight. Her baby brother felt so warm and...well, *heavy.* He smelled of Aussie sunshine and fresh oranges, his favorite fruit. She'd come home to congratulate Grace and Wynn, but this single moment of bliss was better than just about anything.

She balanced Tate on her hip and dropped a dozen kisses on both his cheeks. "You've grown."

"I'm in grade two next year."

"Bet you're loving it."

"I have a good teacher. Her name's Ms. Walton. She's older than my kindie one."

"Older like a grandma?"

He thought about it. "Older like you."

Teagan laughed. "Have you made lots of friends?"

His eyes twinkled. "I have a girlfriend, Tea."

"Awesome. What's her name?"

"Bella Blossom Bird. That's alit-ration." He scratched his head then pointed to the others. "Cole told me that."

"You can learn a lot from your brothers." She winked at Wynn. "All three of them."

Her father was sitting in a high-backed lounger. His hair was more salt than pepper now. His eyes were less lively and more wrinkled at the corners. Beneath the royal-blue sweater, his shoulders were stooped, like they were bearing an enormous weight. Guthrie Hunter was a highly intelligent man. He could see his way through any business challenge and come out on top. Teagan's Georgian-born mother had possessed a different kind of smarts—a wily but also demure way of navigating the trickier barriers that life sometimes threw a person's way.

As Teagan set Tate on his feet, then took his hand and headed over, her chest constricted so much, she could barely get a breath down. She wished her mom were here now. If she could have anything, any wish, it would be to wipe out disease from the world.

As Tate scampered off to his father's side, Teagan

saw the bundle sloped against her father's chest. Honey was wrapped in a soft pink baby blanket, fast asleep.

What an angel.

Teagan kissed her father's cheek as he said welcome home. Then she focused on the baby. Her eyelashes were so long, they brushed her cheeks. Her mouth was the perfect shape and color. A rosebud. One tiny hand was bunched up, peeping outside of the blanket. Her skin was so fine, it was almost translucent.

Cole and Taryn had moved closer.

"Isn't she adorable?" Taryn said quietly. "Such a delicate little thing."

"Lolly Legs," Cole said. "I reckon our cat weighs more."

Teagan caught the teasing tone in her brother's voice but she didn't miss the element of concern, either. Some kids were chubby, like Dex before his growth spurt. Others were naturally smaller…thinner.

Her father asked, "Would you like to have a hold?"

"Oh, I don't want to wake her up."

"She's due a feed about now," he said.

"We should wake her soon then," Taryn said almost gravely.

Teagan looked around at them all. Wynn's expression said, *We'll talk about Honey later when Dad's not around.*

Tate was tugging on Taryn's skirt. "I'm hungry, too."

"Would you like me to peel you another orange?"

He beamed. "Yes, please."

Taking Tate's hand, Taryn said, "Why don't you come into the kitchen and help?"

As the pair headed off, Teagan was careful scooping Honey up. She felt warm and, yes, small and absolutely perfect. What did her life have in store? Teagan brought her baby sister higher and inhaled that sweet baby scent.

It's all about getting up when you're down, Honey. Finding your own way. Trying always to believe in yourself.

"I'm guessing someone must have told you."

Teagan focused on her father. "Told me what, Dad?"

"That Eloise and I...it's not going to work out."

She slid a quick look Cole's way. His eyebrows jumped and everyone except Teagan took their seats again. With Honey in her arms, she preferred to stand.

"I'm sorry," she said. "I'd really hoped you could see a way through."

He propped an elbow on the chair arm and rubbed his brow with that hand. "Eloise is a mess. Drinking more and more. She wanted her own place, so I arranged another nanny for the kids, but they're not getting what they need."

Honey's tiny hand flexed as if to say she agreed.

Teagan asked, "Has the baby gone to all her pediatric appointments?"

"She doesn't have any problems," Taryn said, "although she is in the fifth percentile for weight."

Which meant ninety-five percent of babies her age weighed more.

Teagan was usually happy to help but not control things. Only now, looking down into this precious innocent face, something new and fierce roared up inside her.

Eloise is a mess.

"You can't let Honey stay there," she said. "Babies are so fragile." During that brief window when she'd been pregnant, she'd done so much research. "Their brains and bones need every bit of nourishment."

Cole was nodding. "Dad knows that, Tea."

"He's going to file for custody," Wynn added.

Teagan was taken aback. "For Tate, too?"

"For them both," Wynn confirmed.

Eloise was the farthest thing from a model mother, but these kids must love her nonetheless. Of course, her father would bring in more help to try to compensate. But it wasn't the same as having your mom.

Wynn read her mind. "There's no other way. You said it yourself. That baby deserves the best start in life and Eloise isn't capable of giving her that. It's our responsibility to step in. We need to protect them both, end of story."

The atmosphere was so dark and heavy. The topic needed discussing, but this time was also meant to be about family getting together to celebrate. Teagan tried to lift the mood.

"So, tell me more about this whirlwind wedding," she said to Grace and Wynn. "Was anything planned or did you plunge in on a whim?"

Grace's face brightened. "We started talking one night about all the arrangements a big wedding would involve."

Wynn took his bride's hand. "The following week, we stood before a celebrant and signed the papers."

"And the honeymoon was in Italy?" Teagan asked.

Grace's head rocked back as she sighed. "We are definitely going back."

"Not for a while, though." Wynn winked at his new wife. "I have an office to run."

Cole and Taryn were sitting in a love seat. Now he

put an arm around his wife and sent a manufactured frown his younger brother's way. "Surely they can do without you for another month or so."

Wynn laughed. "That's strange coming from you. Before you met Taryn, you practically slept at the office, weekends included."

Guthrie's bushy eyebrows jumped. "It's good to slow down."

"I haven't slowed down." Cole leaned in to steal a kiss from his wife. "I've simply directed certain passions elsewhere."

"We'll all be calling you Daddy soon."

Cole gave Wynn a deadpan look. "You won't be far behind."

Grace and Wynn turned to each other, a sparkle in their eyes.

When Wynn's phone beeped, he growled but opened the text anyway. "I've funneled down the incoming messages to only those that *seriously can't wait*." After reading, he growled again. "Unbelievable."

Guthrie perked up. "Bad news from New York?"

"Nothing we can't handle with a fly swatter." Sitting back again, Wynn crossed one ankle over a knee. "We did a feature on an actor recently, a guy who used in the '60s. He's in his late seventies now, but still a big name. A reliable source said this man was not only at it again, he was small-time dealing. This is after a very public display of obviously being off his tree."

Suddenly the baby felt heavy in Teagan's arms. Her throat was convulsing. Grace seemed to notice. She got to her feet and took Honey.

"You take my seat," Grace said. "I'm going to enjoy this little sweetie for a while."

Teagan folded into a chair while Guthrie offered a prediction. "So, the actor's got some hotshot lawyer to see if he can drag a few million out of your kitty?"

Now Teagan felt ill. Her father didn't like lawyers at the best of times. He thought they were a necessary evil, perhaps like a lot of the world.

"It seems the actor *did* lawyer up," Wynn said, "but later chickened out. Only goes to show."

Teagan was holding her churning stomach. "Goes to show what?"

"That the story was *fact*. Obviously this actor, Grant Howcroft, panicked when he was caught out. He wanted to file but then saw reason when his junkie brain cleared."

Oh, this was bad. But it could be worse. Teagan didn't know if she wanted to ask.

"Did they say who the lawyer was?"

Wynn shook his head. "Doesn't make any difference." Then the phone beeped again. "Ah. Here we go. He's apparently a big deal in his world. Jacob Stone, Esquire."

A dozen exit strategies whipped through Teagan's mind. But she had always welcomed everyone else's companions, partners. This was awkward but, damn it, she wouldn't tell Jacob to cancel their plans, not after the torment she'd gone through to make the decision. In fact, despite all the down talk about attorneys, she wasn't embarrassed to introduce Jacob as her...friend. And she wasn't going to stew on it for however long before he got here.

"I know Jacob Stone," she said.

Wynn's expression was pinched. "*How?* He's on the other side of the country from you."

"We met at a wedding in LA. He knew the groom. I'm friends with the bride."

Reaching for his coffee, Wynn replied, "Ha. Small world."

Teagan paused. That was exactly what Jacob had said when she'd first mentioned Wynn.

"He's very clued in," she went on. "I think he'd be a good lawyer."

Wynn's expression oozed disinterest. "You don't say."

Grace asked, "How old is this Jacob Stone?"

"Around Wynn's age."

Taryn seemed to have caught on, too. "So you and he talked a lot at the wedding?"

"We talked." Teagan pushed out the rest. "And danced."

Cole's eyebrows swept together as he sat straighter. "Did you see Stone again?"

"As a matter of fact, I met his family on a visit to upstate New York."

Her father's elbow slid off the chair arm while Wynn froze and then blinked once.

"When?" he asked.

"Three weeks ago."

"Have you seen him since?"

"No. No, I haven't."

The hard line of Wynn's mouth eased. "Probably best."

"We have spoken, though. Most recently this morning. I invited him here."

Wynn jerked forward in his chair like a knife had slammed between his shoulder blades. "You didn't."

"I did. Jacob should arrive sometime tomorrow."

Looking around at all the shocked faces, Taryn made her point of view known. "Well, I can't wait to meet him."

"Me, too," Grace said, rocking the baby again at the same time Cole studied Wynn's fuming face and groaned, *"Oh, shit."*

Twelve

Jacob tried to call Teagan— six times now since his flight had landed.

Again. No one picked up.

Sitting in a cab with the engine running, Jacob studied the entrance gates decorated with the sweeping Hunter Enterprises logo. He had three choices. Check into a hotel, fly back home, or buzz that intercom and make a complete dick of himself because if she wasn't answering her phone, there was zero chance of anyone letting him in.

He sat a few seconds longer then threw open the cab door.

Screw it.

"I'll get out here."

The driver's hands stayed on the wheel. "That's one hell of a driveway. You're gonna need a packed lunch."

"I need to stretch my legs." *And clear my head, and drill down on what the hell's going on.*

After receiving that message from Ivy Schluter, he and Teagan had parted on uncertain terms. He'd phoned a couple of times, but Teagan had been hurt when she hadn't heard from him more recently. During yesterday's phone conversation, thankfully they'd gotten back on track. He'd offered to join her during her break Down Under. At the same time, he could meet the family.

Yeah. That was the plan.

The driver had gotten out of the cab and was collecting the luggage while Jacob pulled a bill from his wallet, currency he'd swapped out at the airport exchange.

"Keep the change."

The driver hesitated before accepting the money. "You sure, mate? That's twice the fare."

"I'm sure."

The driver had fallen all over himself to be courteous and chatty to an international visitor who was on his way to meet people who would at best view him as a gate-crasher, and at worst had already made arrangements to have him lynched. Jacob had been about to board his flight at JFK when Teagan phoned to say that her family knew about the defamation lawsuit and the attorney behind it. That was the last time they had spoken.

So had Wynn and the other Hunters convinced her to freeze him out? He'd thought Teagan was stronger than that. Then again, he hadn't forgotten what she'd said about the Hunter clan being protective of its own. Sticking together no matter what.

Jacob was about to try the gate's intercom when a man appeared, strolling along the sidewalk on this side of the ten-foot-high block fence. Big guy, black suit, opaque aviator shades. Not here for the fun. Given what he knew about the attempts on Guthrie Hunter's life, Jacob guessed the man was security.

The guy stopped a good distance away. "Are you looking for someone, sir?"

"Teagan Hunter's expecting me."

The dude turned his head as if to assess the mansion at the same time his iron jaw edged forward. "A friend of hers?"

"That's right. I'm visiting from New York."

"You've been in contact with her recently then."

When Jacob reached for the cell phone inside his jacket, the guy shifted enough for his own jacket to part, revealing a gun holster. *Welcome to the hood.*

Jacob's movements slowed as he extracted his cell and tried to call her again. "I've left messages. She's not picking up."

"Maybe she doesn't want to pick up."

"Maybe there's something wrong with the connection."

"Maybe you'd better move on."

"Maybe you need to *chill.*"

A white Lexus zoomed into the driveway. Teagan jumped out and headed straight over. Jacob wanted to wrap his arms around her, tell her he was happy to see her—despite her not answering his calls and Goon Boy here wanting him to disappear. And that's why his greeting was less than it could have been. He gave her a kiss on the cheek, a tight smile, and then stepped back.

It killed to see her smile fade as she gave him a questioning look.

"I thought I'd be back before you got here," she said.

"My flight was early."

"Have you been trying to call?"

"A couple of times."

She winced. "I'm out of charge."

There. Simple explanation. She didn't hate him. Hadn't thrown him under the bus.

He was pretty sure about that.

She spoke to Goon Boy. "Brandon Powell, this is a friend of mine. Jacob Stone."

Goon Boy didn't remove the shades. Nor did he offer a smile, let alone an apology.

"Yeah. Don't worry about the misunderstanding," Jacob said with just enough *shove it* behind the words. "We've all got jobs to do."

The other man's lip curled in a grin that said, *Bet your ass we do*.

Teagan had returned to her vehicle, so Jacob tossed his bag in the back while she thumbed a button on her remote. The gates fanned back and they headed down the pine-lined drive, leaving Mr. Personality Plus behind.

"Serious security," he said, rubbing the back of his neck.

"Brandon's the head of a PI firm. He's also a long-time friend of the family. One of Cole's mates from his Navy cadet days."

"So, is this a regular thing or because of the trouble?"

After Lanie had brought up the attacks on Guthrie Hunter over dinner, Jacob hadn't found the time to discuss the details with Teagan. He got the feeling she would rather not discuss it now.

"There hasn't been another incident since Cole's wedding," she said. "But no one's been caught yet, either. Until he, or she, is locked away, Dad needs all the help he can get."

"Must be something the super rich have to deal with."

She gave him an unimpressed look. "Thanks for the support."

"No. I didn't mean that the way it sounded." Like, *Boo-hoo, poor you.* "It's just that those with wealth are more visible, and there are a lot of crackpots out there. People with no scruples and even less conscience."

He'd dealt with them more often than he'd like to admit.

Turning into the elaborate porte cochere, which led to a ramp of granite steps and set of soaring front doors, she shut down the engine.

He wanted to lean across and kiss her like he'd dreamed so often of doing these past weeks. But her posture and expression now said, *Not so fast.* He had hoped that with his coming here they could get back to where they'd been before he'd received Ivy's message that day. But his relationship with Teagan was obviously still on shaky ground, and not only because the paternity question was still up in the air. Her family knew about the lawsuit. They were aware he had planned to cut Wynn Hunter off at the corporate knees.

Yesterday, he'd been pumped when Teagan had given him the go-ahead to jump on a plane. Now he couldn't help but wonder if he'd walked into some kind of trap. If her family were less than friendly—if they came down on him like a ton of bricks—would she come to his defense or sit back and watch the fireworks?

From the moment she'd spotted Jacob standing at the gates to the Hunter estate, Teagan's scalp had been tingling. He hadn't looked impressed, and not purely because Brandon Powell had been doing his job and checking the situation out. Jacob's greeting had been stiff, and he hadn't warmed after she explained that her phone had run out of charge. She had no idea that he'd arrived early.

Now as they made their way through the house, headed for the great room where her family had arranged to gather this afternoon, Teagan couldn't shake the sinking feeling. When Jacob hadn't bothered to keep in touch, she'd written their relationship off. But hearing his voice again yesterday had brought back into sharp focus how he made her feel. Alive and desirable. Vulnerable and yet strong. Rather than sticking to her guns and saying goodbye for good, she'd been gripped by an overwhelming need to feel that way again.

Now she was rethinking that, big time.

On top of not being able to contact her and receiving a grilling from Brandon, Jacob must be on edge about those pending paternity test results. She understood why he hoped they were negative. But if he did turn out to be that baby's father, would he still feel angry and cornered or, ultimately, proud?

Teagan couldn't help but be envious. She had even fantasized about that baby being their own. Pointless. Even upsetting. But sometimes, lying awake in bed at night, she just couldn't help it.

And then there was that other matter.

Her family knew that Jacob had planned to drag the Hunter name through the courts. How would Jacob and Wynn handle this face-to-face? She doubted her father or Cole would be overly welcoming, either. Frankly, she couldn't blame them.

On top of all that, everyone was dealing with escalating pressures brought on by another "outsider." It seemed Eloise had really gone off the rails this time. But Teagan felt torn over Guthrie's decision to file for full custody. Of course her little brother and sister needed to be protected, which meant being without their mother most of the time.

That wasn't how it was supposed to be. Teagan still missed her own mom so much. If she were in Eloise's position, she would want to spend every moment with those kids.

So, in hindsight, Jacob being here now was not a good idea. Not a good idea at all. In fact, she wanted to pull up and tell him to just forget the whole damn thing.

But then they were walking into the room and everyone was turning to look their way. Wynn's scowl said it all.

Pressing her damp palms together, Teagan tacked on her smile.

"Everyone, this is Jacob Stone."

She could have kissed Cole for striding over first and putting out his hand. "Good to meet you, Jacob. I'm Cole, the oldest and wisest sibling."

Teagan saw Jacob's expression relax a little when Taryn introduced herself. The woman was all class and heart.

"I'm Taryn. The wise man's wife."

Her dad stood near the fireplace that Eloise had remodeled to overtake the entire wall, all the way up to the vaulted ceiling. Now he came forward.

"I'm Teagan's father. Please call me Guthrie. A funny name, but it's the only one I have."

Jacob shook the older man's hand. "It's a fine name, sir. Good to meet you."

"Tate, my youngest boy, is outside taking advantage of this warm weather and the sandbox. I also have another daughter—" Guthrie winked at Teagan "—a little younger than the first."

"That would be Honey," Jacob said.

Guthrie's gaze sharpened like, *You've done your homework.* "My Honey. That's right."

"I haven't had much experience with babies." Jacob shrugged. "Actually none up to this point. But I look forward to meeting her, too."

Next up was Grace. "I'm the newest addition to the family. Wynn and I took our trip down the aisle just a few weeks ago."

Jacob's smile reached his eyes like he was genuinely pleased for her. "Congratulations. I hope you have many happy years ahead."

And then there was one introduction left. Teagan prayed it wouldn't be a clash of the titans.

"Jacob, this is Wynn," she said. "My brother who works in New York—"

"For Hunter Publications," Wynn said, stepping up, visibly gritting his teeth as he put out his hand. "I believe you work in Manhattan, too."

"Busy place," Jacob said, all too briefly taking Wynn's hand. "It's good to have some time off."

"I'm due back week after next."

Jacob nodded, looked around. "It's a long way from here."

"These days we're all so connected. It's so much easier to keep up to date than, say, fifty years ago."

"Even twenty."

"It's a different world. Nowhere to hide"

Jacob's smile was tight. "Nowhere at all."

Wynn's jaw shifted. "So, Jacob, you're a lawyer. What are you working on at the moment? Any interesting cases?"

Jacob shrugged. "They come up all the time."

"And when there isn't enough evidence to prosecute? I suppose those cases are dropped?"

"There are other reasons a case will be put aside."

"Oh?" Wynn crossed his arms. "Name one."

Jacob's grin was wry. "Are you in need of a lawyer, Wynn?"

"Actually we have an exceptional team. Always prepared to fight. And win."

Teagan groaned. *Enough.* Obviously, Grace thought so, too. Wynn and Jacob weren't talking; they were shaping up. Grace linked an arm through her husband's while Guthrie interjected. He might not approve of the visiting attorney, but thankfully he wasn't making a show of it.

"It really is a full house today," he said. "I'd like you to meet my nephew, Sebastian."

Teagan hadn't realized Sebastian was there. Sitting in a high-backed chair, facing the fire, he got to his feet.

"An attorney, huh?" Sebastian grinned as he ran a hand through his hair. "Wish I'd gotten a law degree."

Jacob arched a brow. "It's not too late. I hear you have fantastic universities in Australia."

Sebastian was the only son of Guthrie's older brother, Talbot, who had left the family business in a huff decades earlier. The families hadn't spoken since that major falling-out, until Sebastian had reached out and reconnected. That side of the family had attended Cole's wedding, and had witnessed the explosion. Now Sebastian was working for Cole, and while he and Jacob talked, Teagan wondered...

If Talbot hadn't opted out of Hunter Enterprises all those years ago, Sebastian would most likely be a CEO now, wielding as much corporate power as his cousins. That was enough reason for a lot of people to be jealous, vengeful. Not that Sebastian ever came across that way. In fact, he was nothing but accommodating.

Someone else Teagan hadn't noticed was pushing to his feet. His hair was thinner and grayer, but she instantly recognized one of her father's oldest friends. Rather than put out his hand, Milo Vennard studied his perpetually unlit pipe as he spoke to Jacob.

"These are interesting times for your country, young man."

Teagan explained, "Professor Vennard is an expert in Marxian economics."

"An ideology growing in popularity," Vennard added, meeting Jacob's gaze. "Particularly in your quarter. Capitalism was always doomed."

Jacob slid both hands into his pants' pockets. "There's certainly a lot of debate going on at the moment."

"Of course," Vennard continued, "there are many influences that affect government and economic policy, although the plight of the working class is rarely one of them. Lawmakers, and *people who administer the law* like yourself, should give a nation its backbone. Have you ever asked yourself what you can do to help the cause?" The man's bushy eyebrows knitted together. "Son, are you part of the problem or the solution?"

Jacob appeared to be forming his words. Before he could reply, however, the professor went on.

"Those at the top are a disease, spreading a palsy that will ultimately dry up every shred of opportunity for the common man for generations to come."

Someone cleared his throat.

"Well, I know *I'm* pretty dry at the moment." Cole tilted his chin toward the bar. "What's your poison, Jacob?"

As the men headed over—with Sebastian eager to fit in and Wynn clearly itching for a fight—Teagan hung back with the girls.

Her gaze on Jacob, Taryn kept her voice low. "Teagan. Uh, *yum*."

Grace was smiling at the boys congregating and talking around the bar. "Wynn did pretty well, considering."

Teagan exhaled. "Well, no one threw an actual punch." So disaster averted. At least for now.

Sighing, Taryn put a palm on her baby-bump belly. "You look so right together."

"You mean despite how he was going to drag Wynn to court?" Teagan asked.

Grace didn't seem concerned. "What is a good love affair without some hurdles? Wynn and I had a couple of doozies to overcome."

"Cole and me, too," Taryn said. "When we met, I thought he was the most arrogant, controlling man on the planet."

"I couldn't see any future for Wynn and me. I had so many doubts." Grace looked at Teagan. "Who are we if not our deepest hang-ups?"

Teagan was thinking back. When she'd met Jacob, he had triggered her, too, but only in the bedroom, and in a very good way. But as well as they got along in that regard, she couldn't imagine her and Jacob getting married, and not simply because of all the ill feelings swirling around the specter of that shelved lawsuit, or the fact that it was way too soon to even consider such a thing.

What about having a family?

Jacob must be on tenterhooks waiting for those paternity results. But if he was like Damon Barringer and wanted a family of his own one day—and not via adoption or surrogacy—Teagan knew from experience that could be a deal breaker. As far as she could tell, there was just no getting around that one.

End of story, close the book and goodnight.

Thirteen

As they left the interrogation room and Teagan led the way down an outside path, through a series of magnificent gardens to one of the Hunter estate's guesthouses, Jacob could barely contain a shudder.

The Rawsons were wealthy folk. Nice home, beautiful property, but, *Geez, Louise*, nothing like this. The estate was on a massive parcel of land overlooking Sydney Harbour, complete with a mansion in every decadent sense of the word… This had to be one of the most expensive pieces of real estate in Australia—perhaps in the world.

My, my, how the überwealthy lived.

As they entered the guesthouse's vast main room, well away from earshot, Teagan made a comment. "Well, Dad was pleasant enough."

Because the old guy had smiled? *Once.* Jacob wasn't

going to whine about it. Guthrie Hunter obviously had other stuff on his mind, like how to dodge the next assassin attempt.

Teagan added, "Wynn was a little defensive."

A little? The fire blazing in Wynn's eyes had said, *I want to rip out your heart and feed it to a lantern fish*— the kind that live at the murky bottom of the ocean and look like a cross between Freddy Krueger and *Dawn of the Dead*.

"The professor friend of your father's is an interesting character," he said, taking in more of the multimillion dollar surroundings before opening a random door that led to a softly lit, marble-clad room that housed a fifty-foot interior lap pool.

Teagan was headed for the other end of the main room. "They've known each other since college."

"They obviously took different approaches to their study of economics." A Marxism economist would probably barf at the accumulation of this kind of monumental personal wealth. "They must have some knockout debates."

"My father and Professor Vennard have different ideas on how the world ought to be run. Dad believes in the dream." She pressed a button on a remote that opened fifteen-foot-high curtains covering four sets of French doors. "Work hard and you'll reap the rewards."

"And the more rules that bend in your favor, the more lucrative those rewards become."

Teagan's eyebrows knitted. "My father—and brothers—are astute businessmen. They contribute. Create jobs. Isn't that something to celebrate?"

"And yet you chose not to join the party." She'd

turned her back on the opportunity to be a part of Hunter Enterprises.

"I prefer a simpler life."

Closing the distance between them, he spread his arms, flipped up his palms and looked around. "Teagan, this is *not* simple."

Her grin was wry. "The Rawsons aren't exactly paupers."

"No. But they give back a lot, and from the heart."

"Right. Because my family doesn't have any philanthropic causes."

"Donations to political connections don't count."

Her beautiful green eyes narrowed. "I don't like this conversation."

As she turned away, he winced and caught her arm, held her back.

"Hey, I'm sorry," he said. "I guess this is harder than I'd thought."

"You mean facing my brother?"

"Not that. *More* than that." He and Teagan had committed to being transparent—honest—so he soldiered on. "I'm used to doing battle with big corporations, not trying to chum up with people who vacation on hundred-foot yachts."

"I seem to recall a flight to New York in a private aircraft."

"C'mon. That plane isn't worth as much as your annual housekeeping bills."

"*My* housekeeping bills?"

"You know what I mean."

"I think I do." She edged away. "Obviously, Wynn is having trouble putting the idea of that lawsuit aside, but let's be honest. You're still champing at the bit to see him pay. Which is funny, because he didn't do anything wrong in the first place."

"You don't know that." He shook his head. "You *can't* know that."

"I know what he told me. He said—"

"Don't tell me." Jacob threw up his hands and turned away. "I don't want to know."

"Exactly."

Jacob was torn down the middle. He wanted to be here, but he didn't need this rock hanging over his head. Ultimately, if Grant Howcroft came back and said he wanted to go through with that lawsuit, Jacob was no longer in a position to help. Wynn Hunter could very well see this visit—at least in part—as a ruse. A way for him to ferret out incriminating information. Or to intimidate him. A judge would see it that way, too.

Which, of course, he had known when he'd suggested that he join Teagan here.

But, boy, it grated having to pass on the opportunity to score a win against an institution that ruined reputations by positing fiction as fact. The other downside of this exercise pained him just as much.

Jacob knew firsthand about coming from nothing and having no one. That reality was the kindling upon which his passion for the law had been built. He wanted to fight the good fight. Level the playing field. Teagan, on the other hand, couldn't possibly know how that felt. Whether or not she espoused being independent, by virtue of her family's Midas-level assets, she was the one percent…privileged in a way normal folk could never dream of.

That wasn't her doing, her fault. At least she wasn't

shoving it down people's throats every chance she got like another woman he knew.

Ivy Schluter.

Teagan was standing by the French doors. The view was a painter's inspiration—a panorama of that bluest of blue harbor with its lazy water traffic and the sweeping shells of Sydney's famed Opera House. Her arms were crossed tightly and her shoulders were squared in that cute polka-dot jumpsuit. Jacob felt like an ass for venting, but he would make up for it now. Not another word about anything other than how happy he was to be spending time with her again. About taking what they had—despite the distractions—to the next level.

He moved across the room and stopped behind her. Then he gazed out over the vista, too.

"I don't think I've seen a more spectacular sight," he said.

She didn't comment, didn't move.

"It must look amazing at night. All the city lights and stars on the water."

He waited again, and finally she spoke.

"My father bought this block of land for my mother. They'd been looking around for a family home—Cole was on the way—and they saw the For Sale sign. The company was going through some hardships at the time. Mom understood they couldn't afford it, but she'd still fallen in love with this view. She'd said it was so close to heaven, you could reach up and swing from the clouds.

"The next week, Dad took her out for a picnic... fried chicken, cheese straws and sweet tea. When he'd stopped here again and said that he'd managed to buy the land, she didn't believe him. So he took the deed from his pocket." She shifted and took a deep breath.

"Whenever he tells that story, Dad says that Mom couldn't stop crying. Tears of happiness, and of thanks. She knew how lucky they were. How privileged. And every single day she gave back, to her family, to the community. She helped others any way she could."

Jacob's heart was in his throat. He let what she'd said sink in before coaxing her to turn around in his arms. Then he waited for her to look up, meet his gaze.

"When I'm here…when I'm home," she said, "I always think about swinging from the clouds. I always think about how happy my mother and father were."

Yesterday on the phone, Jacob had said he couldn't wait to hold her. *Really* hold her. This minute, he wanted that more than anything.

He told her that with his eyes and then with his lips. And he didn't stop telling her until he felt her resistance and doubt ebb away. Until it was just the two of them, standing on a precipice, reaching for the clouds.

Teagan wasn't sure what she was thinking. She only knew how she *felt*. More than anything, that feeling was relief.

Of course this was always going to be tricky. On top of everything else, she'd never brought anyone home to "meet the folks" before. She had never wanted the questions or to face the expectations. She hadn't even brought Damon Barringer over.

After that breakup—and the miscarriage—Teagan had shut off her feelings. Then she'd met Jacob and knew the time was right to put herself out there again. And being with him was *different*. Jacob had a certain edge that made her feel new and exciting, and not only in the bedroom.

And now, as his lips brushed and teased hers, she didn't dwell on why. She simply put her earlier concerns and this disagreement aside, and gave in to being with him again this way. She couldn't have stopped herself if she tried.

He nipped her lower lip, so lightly she could have imagined it.

"I missed you so much." He nuzzled one side of her mouth, her cheek. "You feel so good, Tea. So good."

When his mouth took hers, she leaned in, clung on. And as the sparks grew stronger, her bones turned to jelly and her heart began to pound. The heat of his tongue playing with hers—the subtle pressure of his fingertips toying behind her ear—left her feeling giddy with need. So impatient for more.

He was already slipping the shoestring straps of her jumpsuit off her shoulders. When the kiss deepened and he tugged at the fabric, she left off kneading his chest to get rid of the jumpsuit herself. No bra. Just a pair of lacy boy-cut panties and Keds, which she blindly heeled off and kicked away.

He hooked an arm around her waist and pulled her toward the circular lounge. As he fell back, all contact broke. No one was going to walk past, peep in. Still, Teagan reached for the remote, pressed a button, and the curtains closed across those doors again.

There was still enough natural light to make out his penetrating gaze as he undid each button on his shirt. She came forward, straddled his lap, and then they were kissing again. She took control this time, dragging her fingers back through his hair, caressing his mouth with hers, pressing and rubbing her breasts under his chin.

When she ran out of breath, her lips left his to graze over his jaw to his ear. She whispered, "Are you happy?"

His palms were gliding up over her lace-covered hips. "Trick question, right?"

She took his hand and steered it higher until he was cupping her breast. When he plucked the very tip, she bit her lip to contain the moan. He slid lower until his mouth replaced his hand. Then his tongue looped one way and the other, gently sucking and savoring. All the while, he explored the backs of her thighs, fingers feathering up and down, around and between.

Teagan buried her face in his hair. This was the fantasy she'd had every night since they'd been apart. It was all steam and aching pleasure and breathless anticipation.

Please don't make me wait.

She might have said the words aloud because he took that moment to release the zipper on his pants. She shifted to get up and lead him to the bedroom, but he reached to tug her close again.

"You're not going anywhere," he said around a grin.

Straddling him again, she held on to his shoulders, which were steaming through the shirt. "This could get awkward."

He was looking at her breasts. "Awkward how?"

"Getting your pants out of the way. Mine too. And… other stuff."

Protection.

But he was already fishing around for his wallet, finding and opening a foil wrapper. Then he bucked up and rolled the condom straight on.

As he kissed her again and her arms wrapped around his neck, he trailed his fingertips up the inside of her thigh before burrowing beneath her panties. She felt his smile tease her lips while he slid the crotch to one side. Then the pad of his thumb began to strum. The strokes grew more precise until he found just the right spot and applied just the right pressure.

As the pulse at her core deepened, she broke the kiss, gripped his shoulders again and pressed in. When she started to quiver, began to quake, he brought her hips down until her inner thighs sat flat against the tops of his and all the breath was pushed from her lungs.

He was inside her…*filling* her…unbuttoned, unzipped, but still fully clothed, including his shoes.

Through hair fallen over her eyes, she found his lidded gaze. Then she let her head rock back as she slid both her hands up the hot curves on either side of his neck. As he began to pump, he helped her move. Every thrust sent her that much higher…that much closer… until her climax exploded and the world was raining white hot sparks.

Fourteen

Later that evening when Teagan and Jacob strolled into the dining room, she was taken aback by everyone's expressions. Her stomach pitched and the smile slid from her face.

Who died?

Pushing to his feet, Cole waved them over. "We were discussing a few things."

Taking a seat at the table, Teagan looked around. "Where's Dad?"

Wynn eyed Jacob before tapping the blade of his knife on the tablecloth. "Eloise rang. She wanted the kids back."

"We bundled them up, said goodbye," Cole explained as Teagan and Jacob took their seats. "We didn't want to disturb you guys."

"And if they had to go…" A muscle in Wynn's jaw flexed. "Well, we didn't want to drag it out for Tate."

Teagan was stunned. Was she missing something? "Eloise knows this is a family week, doesn't she?"

Wynn grunted. "I don't think Eloise knows what day it is."

Under the table, Jacob took Teagan's hand. She squeezed back and asked, "Why didn't Dad just say no?"

Ice clicked as Cole swirled his tumbler. "At this point, he thought it best not to upset her."

"Doesn't matter that she upset the kids," Wynn pointed out.

Cole voiced what everyone was thinking. "God, I wish those two had never met. No. I take that back. We have Tate and Honey." He took a gulp and smacked the tumbler back down on the table. "This is going to end badly."

Taryn asked, "You mean with divorce?"

Wynn clarified, "And Eloise scooping up a fortune."

"Money's the least of Dad's worries where she's concerned," Cole pointed out. He turned to Teagan. "We've just found out that she has a boyfriend slash live-in lover. A Kyle Scafe. Brandon's running a deeper check on him. Apparently he's an ex-military man."

Wynn qualified, "One of those soldiers for hire."

"Should Honey and Tate be living with any man other than their father?"

Jacob answered Teagan's question. "Statistics show that minors living with a male not related to them are exponentially more at risk."

While Wynn's eyes burned and narrowed, Cole went

on. "So far, there are no red flags in this guy's history. In fact, his record is exemplary."

"I just need to say—" Wynn hacked out a laugh. "I'm sorry, but I bet my life he's not the first."

When Cole's jaw jutted and he looked down, Teagan was reminded that Eloise had even hit on him once. Unbelievable.

"When is Dad filing the custody papers?" she asked.

"This evening's stunt will bump that up," Cole said. "He'll still have to deal with her, though. Dad wants her in their lives."

So did Teagan. "But if she puts them in danger…"

"Supervised visits." Jacob's shoulders rolled back. "If she has a history, that could be the way to go."

Wynn shook his head. "I can't see Eloise going for that."

"If you can prove that she's toxic," Jacob replied, "you'll have the judge's ear."

"What do you term *proof*?" Wynn's tone was edged with sarcasm. "A *reliable source*?"

He was having a dig at Jacob about the information his reporter had received on Grant Howcroft's alleged drug use.

Jacob didn't take the bait. "That would help. But if you could get solid evidence…photos, police reports, psych evaluations…"

"What if she wants a paternity test?" Cole cringed. "I know Tate is the spitting image of Dad when he was that age. Has all his mannerisms, too. Not that any of that is conclusive. But Honey…?"

"It takes anywhere from a few days to a few weeks to get results back," Jacob said.

"As far as our father is concerned," Wynn pointed out, "Honey is his child. DNA swabs won't change that."

Teagan thought of Jacob's situation, which was obviously very different from her father's. If Jacob's paternity test came back negative, he wouldn't hesitate to walk away. He didn't know the child. Had never met him. Being excluded would leave the way clear for the true father to step up to the plate. Still, blood wasn't necessarily thicker than water. She only had to think of Jacob's past and his relationship with the Rawsons to know that.

As far as Teagan was concerned...she would *die* for those two kids, and her feelings for Honey wouldn't change no matter who her father was. The thought of walking away, never seeing Honey again, made her blood run cold.

"I know we're all concerned about Honey," Grace said. "She doesn't have a voice. But I hate to think of how this time is affecting Tate. What does a six-year-old tell himself when he can see that his family is being torn apart? He's been through enough already."

Taryn gave a thoughtful nod. "There hasn't been any action on the stalker front since the wedding."

Teagan shuddered, remembering how close they had come to losing Tate that day.

"Doesn't mean it's over," Wynn grunted. "I'd like to take them both out of harm's way again until *everything's* sorted."

"Tate has stayed with Dex and me," Teagan told Jacob.

"And I had him over Christmas." Wynn expelled a breath. "Do you know what he told me Christmas Eve? He thought *he* was to blame for his parents' problems."

Cole's eyes suddenly widened and he straightened as he looked past Teagan to the door. *"Dad."*

Teagan turned in her seat. Her father stood on the threshold. He looked beaten. And yet he pasted on a smile as he headed over to the table.

"This isn't much of a celebration for Wynn and Grace, I'm afraid."

Wynn had gotten to his feet to pull out his father's chair while Cole asked, "How are the kids?"

"Eloise decided that she only wanted Honey. Tate came home with me. He's in bed."

Teagan withered inside. Had Tate cried when they'd left his little sister behind? What was wrong with that woman?

She shoved back her chair. "I'll go up and see him."

Her father held up a hand. "He's asleep, sweetheart. Big day."

Wynn returned to his seat. "Was the soldier boyfriend there?"

"He was. Hate to say it, but he was polite. Even concerned."

"And Eloise?" Cole asked.

"She seemed sober. Which almost worries me more. I don't know what to expect next."

None of them did, Teagan thought. Especially poor Tate.

Jacob had been prepared for a challenge. Coming here, he'd wanted to get along with the Hunters, but he hadn't expected to *sympathize* with the family.

They had everything—money, corporate and social power, intelligence. As far as looks went, hell, they could've been the A-list cast from a blockbuster movie.

Or perhaps that comparison was in Jacob's head because someone had mentioned that Dex, the middle brother and head of Hunter Productions in LA, was due to arrive in the next couple of days.

Given the discussion regarding cheating, divorce and custody issues, he'd felt for everyone at that dinner table, including Wynn, who looked so preoccupied and only pushed around the food on his plate. Taryn and Grace tried to lighten the mood with talk about decorating nurseries and honeymoons in Venice. But overall, the dinner was tense, start to finish; plates went away barely touched.

Before heading back to their guest quarters, Teagan told Jacob, "I need to go check on Tate."

"Sure. Of course." He dropped a kiss on her forehead. "I'm totally there if you want me."

She gave him a weary smile and nodded.

They climbed an extravagant sweeping staircase and headed quietly down a long hallway. The bedroom was awash with a soft yellow glow. In one corner, a pack of stuffed animals and plastic dinosaurs stared back at them like a regiment of mini personal guards. The boy lay on his back, one pajama-clad arm dangling over the mattress.

Jacob followed Teagan as she inched closer. When she stopped to gaze down at the sleeping child, her clasped hands tucked under her chin, something in Jacob's chest wrenched so hard, he had to press his lips together to stop the groan. Like the others, he wanted to know this child would be kept safe. But his reaction involved more than that.

At that moment, he got who Teagan Hunter truly was. Loyal, strong and capable of an ocean-deep commitment. Tate and Honey might be going through a hell of a time right now, but their big sister would do *anything* to have them both come out the other side knowing how much they were loved.

When Teagan found his hand, Jacob beat down the urge to clear the emotions crowding his throat. He'd always had a chip on his shoulder about growing up poor and unwanted. Until a few weeks ago, the idea of having a family of his own had never entered his head. Why would it? He'd been raised in a hellhole where discipline meant endless stinging slaps across the ear and going to bed hungry more often than not. Given he had inherited his biological parents' genes, Jacob had never wanted to take even the slightest risk of repeating the pattern.

Later, when they went to bed, Teagan curled into him and he stroked her hair, loving her warmth and her scent. He was still thinking about Tate and those paternity results when she shifted and looked up into his eyes.

"Thank you," she said.

He smiled softly. "What for, baby?"

"For tonight," she said. "For being on our side."

Fifteen

The newlyweds had booked the grand ballroom of an exclusive inner city hotel that boasted dazzling views of the harbor at night. There would be family and select friends, but guests had been warned to refrain from sharing details of the coming event on social media. The key words were *privacy* and *security*. With Brandon Powell's crew on the beat and all arrangements hush-hush, this was set to be a wonderful and—fingers crossed—*uneventful* night.

With five days on their hands until then, Teagan decided to show Jacob the highlights of her hometown. They'd started with the Christmas in July markets at The Rocks, a historic tourist precinct on Sydney Harbour's southern shore. They enjoyed delicious mulled wine, traditional carols and an array of early Yuletide pop-up stores.

The next day, they checked out Bondi. After a walk along the famous stretch of white sand, they sat at a café overlooking the Pacific Ocean and ordered coffee with slices of wattle seed and quandong cake. Quandong, Teagan informed Jacob, was Australia's sweet and tangy native peach.

The following day, they checked out the harbor and an assortment of stops via commuter ferry. They spent most of the day at Sydney's best known theme park— Luna Park—which had its own "Coney Island" complete with a fun house from the 1930s; there were rotating barrels, moving platforms, large sliders and arcade games galore. They rode the hair-raising Wild Mouse roller coaster *three times*. When they left the park at dusk, the entrance—a giant laughing face—was lit up along with all the rides.

On the ferry back, a woman seated nearby heard Jacob's accent and took it upon herself to inform him of the Opera House's history as they passed by the iconic shells, which were illuminated with blown-up moving projections of Aboriginal artwork inspired by the Dreamtime. The woman had been born in 1957, the same year the Opera House architect had won the international design competition.

This was why Teagan would always call Sydney home. The amazing climate, scenery, food and the people. Jacob seemed to feel at home, too. With the wind combing through his hair as he studied the iconic arts center and the sparkling harbor waters while listening to the woman's story, he looked more than interested. Jacob looked like he could truly belong.

Every evening, they hung out with Tate and caught up with family over dinner. Tonight, however, they'd gotten in late and opted for a swim in their very private heated pool.

Wearing an aqua bikini, Teagan dove in first. When she came up for air, somehow Jacob was already right there beside her in the pool, beautiful broad chest and shoulders wet and bare.

She wiped water from her eyes. "How'd you get here so fast?"

"Skill."

She gave his lopsided grin a splash before mermaid diving and swimming away.

Before her accident, Teagan had won plenty of blue ribbons at swim meets. But clearly Jacob had a secret weapon. By the time she got to the other end, there he was again, standing in the shallows, dark hair plastered to his head, upper body glistening, and not the least bit out of breath.

She pretended to pout. "I don't want to race anymore."

His muscled arms looped around her waist. "You want to expend some energy a different way?"

"Oh, you mean like by *talking*?"

His muscles flexed as he grinned and tugged her closer. "Sure. Let's talk."

When he began to twirl them both around, she brought her legs up and locked them around his hips. He was so warm and wet and hard...

"So, what do you want to talk about?" she asked.

"Uh...kangaroos. You piqued my interest at the farm that night."

She remembered well. "I told Lanie to stay away from big reds, our *boxing* kangaroos."

"We didn't come across any this week."

"There are plenty of roos in the Outback—more than

there are people in the whole of Australia. But you won't see them in the city. Some on the fringes, though."

"Around here?"

"Not so much."

He twirled them the other way, smiling when she leaned back until her hair drifted through the water and her legs needed to brace his hips more.

"Interesting fact," she said, tipping back up again. "When they hop, roos only ever use their hind legs together. But when they swim, they kick each leg independently like riding a bike."

"I did not know that." His gaze was on her lips. "What about the pouch?"

"Well, they're marsupials. Babies are born when they're maybe an inch long. They travel up through their mommy's fur then slip into her pouch where they hang out for a few months, fattening up, growing big."

"Sounds like a snug but extremely bumpy ride." He twirled her around again. "And they swim, you say?"

"Very well."

"How are they under water?"

Before she could think that through, he put his mouth to hers and pulled them both down.

Her first reaction was to break off and find some air, but she soon learned that she liked smooching that way. When he brought them both up, her arms were looped around his neck and she was out of breath, in more ways than one.

Humming in her throat, angling her head, she circled the tip of her nose around his. "So, what would you like to discuss now?"

He began to pull her under again. "I think we're all done talking."

* * *

The following evening, upon arriving at Grace and Wynn's party, Teagan spotted the happy couple sitting in a chair swing decorated with reams of airy tulle and fragrant cream roses. Grace's taffeta gown was ice pink, with exquisite beading around the sweetheart neckline. A slit up one side revealed a shorter *after the formalities* skirt underneath. Wynn looked debonair, and so proud, in his tailored tux. As their photographer snapped a few shots, Wynn leaned in to kiss his beaming bride while the guests sent up a collective *"Aww."*

Cole and Taryn made their way over through the small crowd.

"Isn't the room gorgeous?" Taryn said to Teagan. The decor had a Venetian honeymoon theme. There was a miniature bridge with a glistening mock canal and gondola, a bar adorned with *carnevale* masks and a starlit "sky."

"The wedding cake is tiramisu." Taryn looked to Jacob, obviously wanting to include him. "Have you been to Italy, Jacob?"

"Aside from the Bahamas, I haven't been out of the States until now."

He'd had a disadvantaged childhood, but Teagan had assumed that he had traveled since then. The fact that he hadn't hesitated to jump on a flight to join her here for this celebration made her feel even better about buckling to his request, even if she'd suffered a huge case of nerves when he'd first arrived.

As Jacob linked her arm through his, Teagan cast a look around. "Where's Dad?" Cole pointed past the heads and shoulders of the partygoers. Their father was speaking with Milo Vennard. "Oh. I didn't realize the professor was invited."

Cole's grin was slanted. "The other night, Vennard pretty much invited himself. Obviously, he's not finished chewing Dad's ear off about the imminent revolution. He's gotten worse over the years. It's like Hunter Enterprises is responsible for all the economic and social woes of the world. According to him, we need to see the light and make amends."

Watching Guthrie and Vennard, Taryn winced. "Should we rescue him?"

"Dad can take care of himself," Cole said. "At least in that regard."

Looking the part of *on the job* but *under the radar*, in a dark blue suit and matching tie, Brandon Powell strolled up. Cole included his friend in the conversation.

"Has Teagan introduced you to Jacob?"

Straight-faced, Brandon acknowledged Jacob. "We've bumped into each other." With Jacob returning a curt nod, it was obvious the tension between the two men hadn't eased.

Cole was surveying the crowd. "So, everything good?"

With a sweeping, heavy-lidded gaze, Brandon assessed the scene. "Tight as a drum."

"Make sure your guys keep an eye on Tate."

Brandon nodded toward a table where a handful of guests' children were trying on *carnevale* masks. The kids were having fun, but Teagan's mother-hen antennae were quivering.

"Is anyone actually *with* Tate?" she asked.

"Tate has a personal bodyguard assigned." Cole winked at his sister. "Don't worry. We won't let anything happen to him."

Brandon went back to work while Taryn and Cole left to greet friends who had just walked in.

Teagan took the opportunity to bring Jacob up to speed on the details of what led to the current security situation.

"The other weekend, Lanie mentioned the explosion at Cole and Taryn's wedding, but I'm not sure you know the whole story. No one was seriously injured, but Tate came close to being trapped." To being killed. "Wynn found him in the marquee. Another few seconds…"

Jacob bowed his head and swore under his breath. "Poor kid. No wonder…"

Teagan prodded. "No wonder what?"

Jacob's jaw tensed as he looked first at Wynn and Grace and then at Cole and Taryn.

"Well, you all seem so protective of him. I thought I understood why, but that puts your concerns on a whole other level. You had mentioned that Tate stayed with each of you in the States. I have to say, I think that's still a good idea. I think Brandon Powell would even agree with me there."

"Dad and Eloise were still together then. Now they live apart and she's making demands like yesterday when she all of a sudden wanted the kids."

Jacob was frowning…rethinking. "If your father flew either child out of the country without her consent, she could cause all kinds of legal problems for him. And given this ongoing investigation and the continued risk to your father *and* the children…she could have grounds to file for full custody."

Her head was still whirling when Sebastian joined them. After commenting on how lovely the bride looked, he spoke to Teagan.

"My parents pass on their regrets. Talbot hasn't been well. Getting older." With a wry grin, he studied his champagne flute. "Can't turn back time, more's the pity."

Perhaps Jacob could see that Teagan was still wrestling with his legal opinion regarding the possible custody battles. He stepped in with a question.

"Sebastian, you're new to Hunter Broadcasting. How are you enjoying it?"

"It might sound weird, but it feels like home. Of course, I have a lot to learn." Sebastian slid a glance Cole's way. "I know the boss is sick of my questions."

"I'm sure he's not," Teagan assured Sebastian. "You're family."

Sebastian's look said, *That means a lot*. Then he caught sight of Guthrie. "I should go say hi. That Vennard dude's full-on. I feel like the Bolsheviks have their sabers drawn and are marching our way."

When her cousin left, Teagan turned to Jacob. Determined to push those other issues from her mind and enjoy the evening, she ran a fingertip down his black satin lapel. "Are you enjoying yourself?"

His slow, sexy grin drew her in. "There's a dance floor, Tea. And I'm pretty sure they're playing our song."

She laughed. Another cliché. But she really liked the sound of this one.

"I'm in the mood if you are."

"Where you're concerned," he said, "I'm always in the mood."

He was leaning in for a kiss when somewhere behind them an almighty roar went up. Jacob spun around, automatically corralling Teagan behind him, protecting her, while her stomach pitched with panic. All she could think was, *Not again!* and, *Tate!*

But there was no explosion. No flames. No disaster. The roar was the room welcoming newly arrived guests—her brother Dex and his gorgeous fiancée, Shelby.

Releasing that breath, Teagan grabbed Jacob's hand and pulled him over.

"Time to meet more Hunters!"

"What a relief."

From the dance floor, Teagan was watching the last of the guests bid farewell to Grace and Wynn. The lighting was still subdued, the security detail still on duty, but staff were beginning to clear the tables in earnest now. Decorations were coming down.

Jacob pulled her a bit closer as he asked, "What's a relief?"

"That nothing went wrong."

Her hands trailed across his shoulders and then down until they rested on his shirtfront. Jacob could barely contain the *lucky me* groan. He'd had a nice night, but man, he couldn't wait to move on to the next phase of this evening, which involved him and Teagan being completely alone.

"I can say it aloud now. All night, I kept remembering our last Hunter wedding celebration. But, yay." She glanced around again. "No bomb."

"And no Bolshevik revolution."

As her arms curled higher around his neck and she rested her cheek against his shoulder, Jacob recognized something different going on in his brain. It had to do with being this close, the building heat, looking ahead.

Admitting how he felt.

From the get-go, he'd known Teagan was unique—different from any woman he had ever known...even if there were some similarities where Ivy Schluter was concerned. Both Teagan and his ex came from excessive wealth. They were both beauties with trim builds and confident in every way. Come to think of it, they both had green eyes, too.

As his palm rode up and down Teagan's back and he breathed in that signature vanilla scent, Jacob imagined how much calmer he would feel about the *baby* situation with Ivy if he could swap one woman out for the other. That sounded like he was objectifying them. Like he was sexist. That wasn't it at all. It came down to preferring that Teagan be the mother of his child.

That wasn't wrong. That was fact.

Of course, the paternity test could come back negative, in which case those kinds of comparisons would be meaningless. But if the baby *did* turn out to be his, nurturing the bond between father and son would take priority over everything else. He would be two hundred percent committed to being the best dad he possibly could be. That kind of commitment took not only time, but also a truckload of energy.

How would Teagan feel about that?

Perhaps the bigger question was, how did Teagan feel about having kids?

Jacob stilled and his ears pricked up. Someone was calling his and Teagan's names.

The Hunters and a couple of stragglers had congregated around a round table by the mock canal. Standing to one side, Wynn was holding Tate, who was slung against his chest and shoulder, sound asleep. As he and

Teagan joined them, Jacob shored up his smile. When Dex and his fiancée had arrived earlier, he'd enjoyed a brief conversation with the middle Hunter brother. Dex reminded Jacob of Ajax—the cool chick-magnet dude with the dynamite smile. The guy no one could say no to. His *soon to be* wife, Shelby, was a self-assured red-head with an Okie twang and a brand of charm that was sincere and modest. They both made him feel welcome.

As Jacob and Teagan took a seat, Dex looped an arm around the back of Shelby's chair and made an announcement.

"Shelby and I have something to share." Dex looked into his fiancée's smiling eyes. "Time to come clean."

Shelby told the table, "We've set a date for the big day!"

While Guthrie puffed out his chest, Taryn let out a whoop, and Grace got up to fling her arms around the latest Hunter bride-to-be. And Teagan? Was it imagination or did her response sound forced? Jacob thought she looked happy for her brother and Shelby. Her restraint wasn't due to envy. It felt way more personal than that.

As the congratulations kept coming, Teagan slid a look his way. Jacob thought she might be thinking about their future, too. Could she be wondering whether he and Ivy might "do the right thing" and tie the knot for the baby's sake? *If* the baby was his. He just couldn't see it.

Guthrie spoke up. "I feel more *future granddad* vibes heading my way."

"Yeah, we want kids," Grinning from ear to ear, Dex stole a kiss from his future bride. "Why waste my darling's special talents?"

Shelby explained for those who didn't know. "I

worked with children back home in Mountain Ridge, and I was Tate's nanny while he stayed with Dex in LA." She studied Tate, who was still pushing out z's. "I can't wait to be a mom." She sent a wink Taryn's way. "Can't wait to be an auntie, too."

"I have an adorable niece," Grace said. "Tate met her on Christmas Day…the day Wynn proposed."

"Best day of my life," Wynn said.

Grace sighed. "The older you get, the more you realize children are what makes it all worthwhile. They're what's most important." She looked at Jacob. "Do you have any nieces or nephews, Jacob?"

"My brothers are nowhere near settling down. My sister…" He thought back. "I can't remember if she's ever had a boyfriend. I mean, I'm pretty sure she likes boys."

Teagan gave him a dry look. "Lanie definitely likes boys."

After meeting his sister once, how could Teagan be so sure? Not that it mattered. He loved his sister. He loved all his family, like Teagan so clearly loved hers.

The Vennard dude was sitting at the table, too. Waving that unlit pipe around his head, he put in his two intellectual, and disconnected, cents' worth now.

"The children of future generations are in dire straits. Goliath corporations have taken over, debasing the working wage, destroying the environment, wiping out the future for those who breathe the fetid air of the decadently privileged." He pointed the pipe Jacob's way. "The gap between the elite and lower classes is fast evaporating. Soon the homeless will multiply to staggering levels in countries that once bragged about high standards of living."

Everyone was looking either down or away. Great that this man had a passion but, sorry, this was not the place to express it. He was completely over-the-top and out-of-bounds. Still, Jacob had a question. He was living on Easy Street now, but he could never forget the lack of food and opportunity growing up. So many kids were in that same boat today.

"If you were in charge, Professor Vennard, what would be your first command? How would *you* begin to turn it all around?"

Jacob didn't miss Guthrie's grunt of disapproval. Hunter Enterprises was one of those evil Goliath corporations Vennard was ranting about. The family had accrued a massive fortune and, Jacob was sure, saw no reason for change. And the other Hunter men? Cole, Wynn and Dex were looking straight at Jacob as if to ask, *Whose side are you on, Stone?*

"The first thing?" Vennard's eyes gleamed. "I would reclaim all the wealth, those bulging bank accounts, the hoarded property."

Jacob was listening. "How would you do that?"

Vennard gripped his pipe tighter. "Let's assume we had a favorable change of government. The transfer could be achieved quite peacefully."

Cole scratched his ear. "If you're talking about a revolution, they're rarely peaceful."

"Let there be violence then!" Vennard's face was suddenly red. His gaze was burning. "Armies are growing in strength as we speak, waiting in the wings, becoming bolder and smarter, beginning at last to fight back. And, by God, we will *win*."

Jacob had a clear view of the entire room, including the main entrance. Brandon Powell had stood there surveying the area as guests filed out. Now he moved closer, sending eye signals to his men.

As Jacob had told Teagan, he didn't deal in criminal law, but he had friends who did. Most murders were committed not by strangers but by people known to the deceased. Powell's guys had been thorough when searching guests entering this room. Vennard wasn't armed as such. But his walking stick, Jacob knew, could cause some damage if it came down with enough force. Individuals could die from a sharp object—like a pipe—rammed through an eye socket or throat.

"The elite have used violence in all its forms through-out history," Vennard went on. "They will use any means available to subdue what they term 'the mob.'" When Sebastian cleared his throat, uncomfortable, Vennard spoke directly to him. "*You* know there are people who don't play by the rules. Who are determined to seize power and shut others out."

When Sebastian looked to his cousins around the table for help, Cole spoke up again.

"If you're referring to Hunter Enterprises, Professor, we're all about being fair, offering opportunities. You've worked there a few months now, Sebastian. Tell the professor your experience."

Sebastian's mouth tightened as he shrugged. "It's a great place to work."

Vennard placed his cane on the table as he sat forward. "This boy is reluctant to share his true feelings." With a caring note in his voice now, he addressed Sebastian again. "Decades ago, your father was squeezed out of the Hunter company, wasn't he, son? You should have been perched at the top of the tree now. Instead you are begging for crumbs."

Guthrie intervened. "That's enough, Milo."

Quite enough. Jacob had no objections to people holding fast to their beliefs—philosophical, personal, whatever. He even agreed with some aspects of Vennard's argument. These days the imbalance between haves and have-nots was staggering. But Jacob was only thinking about Guthrie's safety now.

Vennard's grip on his cane tightened even as he cajoled. Looking at Sebastian, he said, "Let the boy answer."

Sebastian cleared his throat again. "From what I know," he began, "you're right. My father was squeezed out in those early years."

Cole coughed out a humorless laugh. "That's not true. They couldn't agree on—"

"Oh, c'mon. It *is* true. My father still feels betrayed." Sebastian's chin wrenched higher. "And, frankly, I don't blame him. I'd be spitting mad, too."

Jacob was concentrating on Brandon now. He was closing the distance, looking to Cole for a sign to intervene. The situation was going downhill fast.

"It must be hard working alongside me then," Cole replied.

Sebastian's smile didn't quite reach his eyes. "I have great faith it will all even out in the end."

Shooting to his feet, Vennard cried out, "Equality! Liberty!" He swung the cane above his head. "Fraternity against tyranny!"

Cole and Jacob leaped up at the same time Brandon swept in, other guards close behind. As they wrestled with the man, Guthrie, dazed and hurt, stared up at his old friend.

Vennard was struggling, cursing at the brothers. "Get your Fascist hands off me! You can't hold us back."

Tate was stirring awake. While Wynn hurried him away from the commotion, a weary Guthrie made it to his feet.

"Milo…my friend…you're not in your right mind."

"What is genuine is proved in the fire." Vennard's eyes filled with frenzied tears. "We have nothing to lose but our chains."

As Milo Vennard was ushered away, Guthrie muttered to himself again. "He's not well…not well."

Cole sliced a hand through the air. "You can't have that man around anymore. That's the end of it."

"Of course," Guthrie grumbled. "I just wonder…"

"Whether he's been behind the threats on your life?" Dex's eyes narrowed. "He was at the wedding. He mentioned an army waiting in the wings. Does he have connections that are capable of pulling off an explosion?"

"That very first incident, when I was run off the road… I had just spoken to Milo." Guthrie shuddered. "God save us all from fanatics."

Jacob made a point. "The victors in history decide who the fanatics are."

Dex laughed. "You *agree* with Vennard's ranting?"

Jacob thought about his abject poverty growing up. "I think it's fair to say that I have more experience with Vennard's ideas about injustice than you ever could."

Jacob was aware of Teagan sitting beside him, stiff. He moved to take her hand under the table. As soon as their fingers touched, she pulled away.

Sebastian nodded to those at the table. "I'm calling it a night." He pasted on a smile for Grace's sake. "Again, congratulations to you both."

When Sebastian was gone, those left shared a look.

Dex kicked the conversation off. "Sebastian's take on our families' history was an eye-opener."

Guthrie's shoulders slumped further. "I had no idea he was so resentful."

Cole was standing behind his father's chair. "Sebastian appeared on the scene after the attacks began, Dad."

"He was there at your wedding, Cole," Dex added. "And he jumped at the chance to work at Hunter Broadcasting. He's inside now."

Cole speculated. "Keeping his enemy closer?"

Teagan repeated Sebastian's comment. "It will all even out in the end."

Someone's phone was beeping. When Guthrie pulled out his cell, Cole groaned. "Whoever that is can wait."

But Guthrie was already studying the screen.

"It's Eloise," he said and connected.

Jacob didn't think Guthrie's face could get any paler. By the time he disconnected, the older man was visibly shaken. He looked at each of his children and ground out the latest news.

"We need to go. That was Eloise's new beau. She's in hospital. Honey's there, too."

Sixteen

When the Hunters arrived at North Sydney General Hospital, Eloise's lover was waiting. The tall, well-built tank of a man stood by the visitor lounge windows, his hands stuffed into his jeans' pockets as he gazed out at the twinkling city skyline.

Earlier, Kyle Scafe had called on Eloise's phone to inform Guthrie that his estranged wife had suffered head injuries. Apparently, someone from child protection services had taken Honey away.

As they'd rushed from Wynn and Grace's party, Cole had wasted no time contacting the hospital. No one could say whether Honey had been injured, too.

While Taryn, Shelby and Grace had taken Tate home, the rest of the family had piled into Cole's vehicle. Now, like everyone else, Teagan had questions for Kyle Scafe. How had Eloise hit her head? Where was Honey when it happened? Where precisely was the baby now?

Kyle heard them enter the lounge. He edged around, took his hands from his pockets and greeted them with a thousand-yard stare. Teagan had assumed he would be agitated. He only looked detached.

"I'm sorry to meet you under these circumstances," he said as though reciting a line from a play.

Cole, Dex and Wynn stood beside their father while Guthrie stepped forward and demanded, "Is my daughter still on the premises?"

Kyle Scafe's broad brow wrinkled like he was trying to think. "I have no idea."

"I'll go find some answers," Dex told his brothers.

He was about to head off when a doctor joined them. "Who do I speak with about Eloise Hunter?" she asked.

Guthrie straightened. "I'm her husband."

The doctor lowered her folder. "When your wife was brought in, she was under the influence of alcohol. Mrs. Hunter suffered a blow to the head. No fractures, but abrasions and bruising. I've ordered an MRI to check for bleeding on the brain."

Guthrie was nodding. "And my daughter? The baby?"

Kyle moved closer. "I was with Eloise when it happened. When we got here, Honey was taken away."

The doctor looked between the two men. "I'm sure CPS have questions for you both. I'll let the representative know you're here." She spoke to Guthrie. "You can see your wife now. She's awake."

Guthrie exhaled. "Thank you."

As they all moved forward, the doctor held up a hand. "Only Mr. Hunter at this time."

As Guthrie followed the doctor down the hall, Teagan felt the atmosphere in the waiting lounge turn from strained to verging on lethal. No one took a seat while a dazed Kyle ran a hand through his dirty-blond hair.

"Eloise obviously has a problem," he said.

Cole folded his arms. "At least one."

"I've seen her drink before, but never around the kids." Kyle's unshaven jaw clenched as his walnut-size Adam's apple bobbed up and down. "I hadn't realized that she'd downed almost the entire bottle of gin. The last time she came back from the bathroom, she was swaying."

Teagan asked, "Where was the baby?"

"With me, asleep in her playpen."

"And the full-time nanny my father pays for?"

"Eloise sacked her earlier today."

Wynn set his fists low on his hips. "What happened next?"

"I got up to help Ellie," Kyle said, "but she pulled back, fell and—" He smacked his head to demonstrate. "The ambulance only took a few minutes."

The doctor appeared again. "The family can go through. The baby is with her parents now."

The doctor provided a room number. As she walked off, Kyle started after her.

Dex blocked his way. "Sorry. She said family."

Eloise's lover's face turned dark and hard. His hands clenched but he obviously thought better of starting anything, particularly with all three brothers ready to take him on if need be.

Leaving Kyle behind, they all found the room and edged inside. When Teagan saw Eloise, she winced. Eloise's eyes were puffy and bruised. The amount of bandage wound around her head was daunting. But no one asked how she was. Instead they gravitated to their father's side. Guthrie was holding the baby.

Eloise sounded groggy. Whiny. Still sloshed.

"I'm sorry...so sorry..."

Teagan had always let her stepmother's questionable behavior slide. She'd never wanted to cause or add to any ill feelings. This time Eloise had gone too far.

Teagan felt her nostrils flare as she growled, "You disgust me."

Eloise's swollen eyes widened. "Tea, sweetie, don't say that. I can't take that kinda talk."

Keeping her eyes on the baby, Teagan held up a hand. "I'm only thinking about Honey and Tate now."

Eloise tried to sit up. "Well, Honey's not hurt, is she?"

"Next time, she could be," Dex said.

"You're forgettin'—" Eloise's chin rose "—I'm that child's mama."

Feeling ill, Teagan groaned. "You don't deserve to be."

Standing behind her, Jacob held Teagan's shoulders—his touch warm, strong and supportive. But she hadn't forgotten his earlier comments, which made crystal clear his opinion of her family. His questions had helped drive that earlier conversation off a cliff. *If you were in charge, Professor Vennard, what would be your first command? How would you begin to turn it around?*

And she had more to worry about now.

Eloise's eyes welled up as she sank back onto the pillow. "I just feel so lost. So afraid. I don't know what to do."

"Here's a start," Wynn said. "Give up the bottle."

As a tear ran down her cheek, Eloise begged Guthrie. "I want to change. I want to be a better mother." Her voice cracked. "I *need* to be a better wife."

"You've said that before." Guthrie shook his head. "This can't go on."

"No. No, it can't." Eloise closed her eyes and held her bandaged brow like she was trying to remember. "You wanted me to go to rehab. I'm ready. Ready tonight. Right now."

Honey was wide awake, her big blue eyes darting between each of their faces as if she were trying to keep up with the conversation. Teagan wanted to tell her, *You'll never have to worry again. We'll protect you from now on, I promise.*

"It's not that easy anymore," Guthrie told his wife. "The authorities are involved now."

Eloise began to sob, maybe for real, maybe for show. "One more chance. Oh, Guthrie. I want to go home."

Cole had a question. "What about the man who brought you here? What will Kyle Scafe have to say about that?"

"Well, Kyle will just have to understand." She reached out an arm, fingers splayed wide. "Bring Honey to me. I want to tell her I'm sorry."

Guthrie hesitated before his mouth tightened and he moved over to the bed. Teagan felt for her father. He had to protect his children. To do that, he needed to keep them away from their mother. Come Monday, she knew he would file for full custody. From then on, any visits with Eloise would be supervised.

As Eloise fawned over Honey and her husband, the others turned to leave them alone.

Someone stood blocking the doorway.

"Is Ellie all right?" Kyle asked, trying to see into the room. "I heard crying."

Cole crowded the man back. "I'm sure Eloise will be fine."

Kyle tried again to see past the wall of Hunter brothers. "I need to see Ellie. Just a minute or two."

Dex held up a hand. "Buddy, you need to leave."

Kyle took a moment before stepping back. When the brothers were out of the way, however, the ex-military man lunged into the room.

"Kyle!" Eloise's mouth trembled with an uncertain smile. "I didn't know you were still here."

Kyle's head went back. "Where the hell *else* would I be?"

As Guthrie handed the baby to Teagan, a nurse, who had obviously heard the commotion, trounced in.

"Okay." She pointed at the doorway. "Everyone needs to leave now."

But Kyle wouldn't budge. He was staring at Eloise, slowly shaking his head as he murmured, "I'm not leaving, Ellie. I'm not."

Wynn tried to make the man see reason. "Let's not make a scene. Think of the baby."

Kyle only wanted to hear from Eloise. His expression was so pained, he looked as if his insides were being ripped out. "You're not going back to him, are you?"

"You need to go." When the nurse put her hand on Kyle's arm, he flung her off and said again, low but also firm, "Ellie, you can't go back."

Eloise waved her hand in the air dismissively. "We'll talk later. Listen to the lady. You need to go now."

Kyle's pale eyes were glistening. "You don't love him. You've told me that a thousand times." Then he turned his attention to Guthrie. His voice was thick, on the verge of breaking. "You need to be out of her life."

Guthrie backed up. "Calm down, son."

"You just won't *go*!"

"I'm getting security," Cole said.

But as he turned, Kyle exploded and sucker punched Cole from behind. At the same time, Dex caught Cole as he fell forward. Wynn, who was at the door, called out for security, then shot back into the room to help his father. Jacob got there first.

He grabbed Kyle from behind. As the man swung around, Jacob jabbed him low and hard in the ribs. When Kyle doubled over, Jacob delivered a swift uppercut to the jaw. Kyle was stumbling back when two security men shot inside the room.

As the uniformed men each grabbed an arm, Kyle shook his head and, appearing dazed again, looked around. Then he drew in a breath, straightened to his full height and made an announcement.

"I want a lawyer."

Seventeen

"Sorry to bother you guys so early," Wynn said, stepping inside the guesthouse the next morning, "but I figure you'd want to know. Kyle Scafe confessed to the attempts on Dad's life."

All the breath left Teagan's lungs at the same time Jacob put a bracing arm around her. She was shaking.

"Thank God, thank God, it's finally over."

The previous evening, fingers had been pointed at Milo Vennard and then at Sebastian. But after Kyle had asked for a lawyer at the hospital, people began to seriously wonder. Later, gathered back at the Hunter estate, everyone had talked into the early hours. The general consensus was that Eloise's live-in lover was a far more likely suspect, and they'd been right.

"Something else." Wynn arched a brow. "Kyle thinks he's Honey's father."

Teagan held her sick stomach. "So the affair's been going on a while."

"Apparently there was a one-night stand. Eloise didn't want to see him again, but Kyle grew more and more obsessed. He started out wanting to scare Dad. Some macho crap about needing to prove to Eloise what a weak man she'd married. They only got back together when Eloise and Dad separated."

Jacob asked, "How did he organize the explosion at the wedding?"

"He got friendly with the DJ before the event and managed to slip the device in with the equipment. Brandon's looking into how that could have happened on his watch." Wynn sucked in air between his teeth. "I would like to know, too."

"Let's just be grateful more harm wasn't done," Teagan said.

Whenever she thought of how close Tate had come to being caught in those flames, she got goose bumps.

Wynn stuck his hand into his pocket. "Another thing. Dad's taking a paternity test. Not that it will make any difference. Kyle Scafe will be put away for a very long time and those results will remain private."

"And Honey," Teagan said, "will stay with us."

From the day Honey was born, she had fallen in love with that little girl. Paternity results could never change that. Honey was family and always would be.

Wynn smiled at his sister. "Grace and I are heading off today to see friends who couldn't make the party. We'll be back later in the week," he said, wrapping up the conversation.

"I'm flying out tomorrow," Jacob said.

Wynn studied the other man and put out his hand.

"Thanks for helping out last night. I thought Kyle might break your jaw. You ended up almost breaking his. You must've taken self-defense lessons."

Accepting Wynn's hand, Jacob admitted, "Every day for the first fourteen years of my life."

When she and Jacob were alone again, Teagan moved to the window view. Looking out at the harbor, she hugged herself tight.

"Dad will really need support now." More than ever.

Jacob joined her. "More visits home?"

"I've been thinking. I'm going to put the gym on the market. Come back here to live for a while."

Jacob looked at her like she'd said she'd eaten razor blades for lunch. "Back to Australia? Half a world away?"

"It's not half a world away to me. I lived here most of my life."

"You said you didn't *like* your life."

Uh, no. "I said I wanted to do my own thing. Now I want to do that in Sydney rather than Seattle."

Their gazes were still locked when Jacob's phone pinged.

"You should get that," she said.

"We're talking."

She raised a brow. "Read the message."

He hesitated before digging out his phone. As his eyes shut tight and he seemed to curl into himself, Teagan watched the color drain from his face.

"What happened?" She gripped his arm. "Jacob, what's wrong?"

"That was the paternity testing company. The results…they're *positive*. The baby's mine." His shoulders pulled back as he sucked in a sharp breath and peered into her eyes. "I'm a father."

Teagan's mouth dropped open. She'd known this was a possibility, but deep down she'd believed those results would be negative. Clearly, Jacob had felt the same way.

So what did she do now? Congratulate him? Saying sorry didn't fit.

Jacob was staring off…looking ahead.

"It's weird," he said. "I've only ever seen photos, but these past weeks I've thought so much about how my life would change if he actually were mine. I'd be watching him grow into a man, guiding him along the way. Making sure he gets a solid education. Being there at his wedding. But I honestly didn't think it would turn out like that."

Jacob looked so thrown. Who wouldn't be? Still, Teagan couldn't help but wish this revelation belonged to her…that someone had passed on the news that *she* was a parent.

"He's a lucky boy to have you and the Rawsons behind him."

Jacob seemed to wither at the idea of telling his family. Then he took both her hands in his and searched her eyes.

"Have you thought about children, Tea? Having a family?"

Not so long ago, she hadn't thought of anything else. But now she needed to come at the question from a more impersonal point of view.

"I think most people think about that on some level, at some time."

"Seeing how you are with Tate and Honey… I think you'd make a great mom."

His eyes shone in a way she hadn't seen before. Her throat got so choked up, she wondered if she could push out the words.

"I think so, too."

He cupped her cheek. "If you do move back home…" He smiled. "Well, we'll just need to get inventive."

Oh, Jacob. "It'll take more than that."

"*Whatever* it takes, because the way I feel when I'm with you…it's the way I felt when I went to live with the Rawsons. I feel safe, Tea. I feel *home*. Maybe we could build on that together."

Her stomach was tied up in knots. They'd agreed to be transparent, but she had held on to one deep, dark secret. Now she couldn't keep it back.

"You know about my scar. That childhood accident."

He nodded. "You fell off a bike."

"I had so many surgeries, so much time off school. Later I was told I would never conceive."

His eyes widened before he took a breath and nodded. "That had to be a shock."

"It was more of a shock when I *did* conceive."

"Wait. You're saying you have a child?"

"I miscarried. The worst day of my life." She was going to be a mom —then suddenly she wasn't.

He didn't hesitate. He bundled her up in his arms and murmured against her ear, "Tea… I'm so sorry."

She soaked in the warmth and for the first time wasn't flooded by images of blood on the bathroom floor when she thought of that night. Still, the upshot was the same. "I will never carry a baby to its full term."

She drew away and held his gaze, waiting for a response.

"I want you to know," he began, "that doesn't make any difference to me. Being a father was never on my agenda. My old man was a complete douche. I hate that I have his genes. I never wanted to pass them on. I never wanted to be put in a position where I could make the same mistakes."

Teagan was blown away—*not* in a good way.

"But you *have* passed them on. You have a son now."

"I know. I *know*. I guess what I'm trying to say is… I'm totally on board with stopping at one."

She should have breathed out a sigh of relief. It sounded like a win-win all around. And yet seeing the uncompromising gleam in his eyes only made the knots in Teagan's stomach twist tighter.

Jacob wanted to do better than his own father had done. But if a person had never wanted a child—if he had pretty much decided to renounce every paternal bone in his body…

How on earth would this relationship between father and son end?

A voice in her head kept whispering, *Maybe not so well.*

Eighteen

A week later, back in Seattle, she took a call from New York. The first thing Jacob said was, *"I miss you so much, baby,"* and Teagan melted inside.

It felt so good to hear his voice again. It brought back how passionate and alive he made her feel. It also made her wish there was some way to fix what was missing between them. Some way to make this work.

"I had to let you know," Jacob said, "Grant Howcroft OD'd yesterday."

A chill crept up her spine. Howcroft was the actor who'd wanted to sue Hunter Publications for defamation over reporting on his use of drugs.

"He died?"

"No, but apparently authorities found a huge stash at his home." Jacob paused. "Go ahead. Say, 'I told you so.'"

"I'm just glad he gets another chance." She added, "And, yes, I'm happy for Wynn."

Her brother's reputation remained firmly intact, as it should. As she'd always known it would.

Jacob changed the subject. "So, what are you up to?"

Dragging her teeth over her lower lip, Teagan took in the scene beyond her office window where scores of enthusiastic clients were enjoying the gym's main workout area.

"Actually, I put the gym on the market."

"Oh. So, you're going ahead with it then?"

"It could take a while to sell."

She waited for him to mention her intended move back to Sydney. When he didn't, she let it slide, too.

"How's your dad doing?" he asked. "Have you heard?"

"With Kyle Scafe locked up until the trial, he's feeling relieved that he doesn't have to look over his shoulder anymore."

"And Eloise?"

"She's in treatment, so fingers crossed there."

Given the circumstances surrounding her stay in the hospital, hopefully Eloise would be motivated enough to turn herself around. Miracles sometimes happened; Teagan truly wanted to believe that.

"And the kids?"

"I spoke to Tate last night. He says that he loves the new nanny Dad hired, and Honey does, too, so I shouldn't worry about them."

Jacob chuckled. "He's a good boy."

Yeah. "He's the best."

"So, what are you doing this weekend?" His tone was purposely upbeat. "I can fly out. Or we can meet midway. How about Colorado? There's a bluegrass fest happening. And I know a great place to stay." He groaned like he was caught between pleasure and pain. "A week's too damn long not to have you in my arms."

Teagan closed her eyes. Every part of her ached to have him close again, too. She wanted his mouth covering hers, his hard heat pressing in. But these past few days she'd had more time to think things through. She felt sick to her stomach having to say it, but there was no way to sugarcoat.

She took a deep breath and forced the words out.

"Jacob, I don't think this is going to work."

The silence was deafening. *Agonizing.* It went on for so long, she wasn't certain he was still there.

"Jacob?"

"Is it because of the distance?" His voice was so raw.

"That's a factor." But hardly the deal breaker.

"We can make that work. Some weekends…vacation time…"

"You have a child to consider now."

And wasn't it telling that she was the one who had to mention that? If she was in his place, a new parent, no one would be able to shut her up.

Jacob sounded uncertain now. "Does that make a difference to how you feel about us?"

She shut the window blinds and withered into a chair. "I don't want to get in the way."

"If you need time, Tea, I'll wait."

"Jacob, that wouldn't be fair."

"On who?"

"You need time to focus on that baby." *You need to make sure that works, not us.*

While another silence stretched out between them,

the nerves in Teagan's stomach squeezed and squeezed. She'd broken up with Damon because she hadn't been able to give him the family he'd wanted. Jacob had never wanted children—that fit with her physical but not her emotional makeup. She *loved* kids. And she worried that Jacob's ambivalence would taint his relationship with his son, perhaps deeply.

She couldn't fix that, or be a part of it. Inevitably, it would tear her, and them, apart.

"You're right," he said finally. "I've got a full plate at the moment. You do, too."

Tears were stinging the backs of her eyes. She hated that this was happening, but she just couldn't see any other way.

"There's a lot going on," she agreed.

He cleared his throat. She imagined him running a hand through his hair.

"So, best of luck with selling the gym."

Dying inside, she held the phone closer to her ear. "All the best with…everything."

She was thinking of something more to round off the goodbyes. It all seemed so abrupt. So final. But then it was too late.

Jacob was already gone.

Nineteen

"I know this must be a surprise."

Teagan gaped at the woman standing at High Tea Gym's entrance and admitted, "That's the understatement of the year."

"I was in town for an event," Lanie Rawson said, wearing her jodhpurs and knee-high boots like the best socialites wore Givenchy. "We need to talk."

Teagan wanted to roll her eyes. *Stop with the intimidation tactics already.*

"You obviously haven't heard," Teagan replied. "Jacob and I aren't seeing each other anymore."

They'd said goodbye six long weeks ago. It still hurt, and she still wondered, especially lying awake late at night. But her decision to step away was the right one. Jacob had an important job ahead of him. He needed to work all his issues out for himself. It wouldn't help anyone, including that baby, for her to be involved.

As Lanie looked around, that storm of long brunette hair swished across her shoulders. The main workout area was filled with clients cycling, running, pumping weights. The music was pumping, too. "Can we go somewhere more private to talk?"

What could they possibly have to talk about? What was the point? But then Teagan thought back to how Jacob and Wynn's relationship had started off—they'd been like two bee-stung bulls ready to charge. By the end of their Sydney visit, the pair were shaking hands and meaning it. She wouldn't turn Jacob's sister away now without giving her some time.

Then she'd kick her out.

They went into Teagan's office and took seats around the small conference table. Lanie swept back her hair, clasped her hands on the tabletop and pinned Teagan with a no-holds-barred look.

"First," she began, "I want to apologize. When you were at the farm, I was rude."

Teagan almost spluttered. *Well, yeah.*

"I was angry," Lanie went on. "Worried that Jacob would be hurt again."

Because of his relationship with Ivy Schluter?

"Lanie, you don't even know me."

The other woman paused and then came at it from a different angle.

"We were all surprised to learn that Jacob was a father," she said. "I know he was, too. Until recently, it was the furthest thing from his mind. But when the results came in, there was never any doubt that the rest of the family would accept and love Benson." A thoughtful smile softened her gaze. "He's the most adorable little boy. You can't imagine."

Teagan *could* imagine, because she'd felt the same way when Tate had been born. Instantly smitten. One hundred percent committed. That went for Honey, as well.

"But the mother." Lanie visibly shuddered. "When Jacob and Ivy dated, he was in a constant spin. She was either smoldering or colder than a January frost. Ivy comes from big money and happily admits that it's all about her. Jacob was not a priority. I felt like I was watching a replay of how he must have felt growing up. Entirely dispensable." Lanie's head angled. "You know the story?"

Teagan nodded. A drug-addicted mother and criminal deadbeat dad. No love. No *anything*. Lanie was right. As a child, Jacob must have felt thrown away.

"Naturally, Jacob had baggage to burn," Lanie went on. "But he had faith in my father, and he grew to trust us all. Ivy came along at precisely the wrong time when he was ready to trust on a different level. She reeled him in, spat him out, reeled him in again. Their breakup hit him hard. When Jacob said he was bringing someone new home to meet the family, I was so glad to hear excitement in his voice again. Ivy was finally a sulky blip in his rearview mirror. Then, like any normal person, I searched you on the internet. I learned that Teagan Hunter was the daughter of one of the top three wealthiest men in Australia. Naturally, I thought, *Here we go again*. Another überrich bitch wanting to jerk my brother's heartstrings. And when I met you, frankly, you looked the part."

Teagan's smile was saccharine sweet.

Don't respond.

"I was bursting to tell you that Jacob didn't need that kind of crap again. I wanted you gone. And if you needed a push, no skin off my nose."

"I'm sure Jacob can look after his own affairs." *In every sense of the word.*

As Lanie leaned forward, a dark wave fell over her eyes. "You have siblings, Teagan. If they were vulnerable, wouldn't you try to protect them?"

Tate and Honey's faces flashed into Teagan's mind. With their mother in rehab, their parents' marriage on life support…

Would she try to protect her siblings?

Teagan lifted her chin. "In a heartbeat."

The heat in Lanie's eyes cooled a few degrees and she settled back in her seat. "Do you know that Jacob has the baby every weekend now?"

Teagan blinked. "Jacob asked for that?"

"Ivy suggested it. Almost *demanded* it. Apparently her beauty sleep has suffered terribly, poor dear. Anyway, Jacob's bought a place in Connecticut and works from home if Ivy wants another day or two's reprieve." Lanie's gaze drifted off. "I'm sure Jacob loves that little boy…but he's so torn. He *wants* to be happy." Her gaze locked with Teagan's again. "He just misses you so much."

Teagan's stomach pitched. "He told you that?"

Lanie nodded then let out a sigh. "For what it's worth, I don't think you're another version of Ivy. You're not just *me me me*. I think your breakup has to do with Jacob becoming a father out of the blue. But no matter how much you try to hide it, I can see in your eyes that you miss him, too. So maybe there's a chance…" Her smile was wan. "Anyway, I had to try."

Lanie had admitted she'd been wrong about her. Teagan had been wrong about Lanie, too. Her behavior at the Rawsons' farm had had nothing to do with being jealous. Lanie wasn't in love with her stepbrother. She was a caring sister who had taken a chance in coming here today for Jacob's sake.

After the women exchanged numbers and said goodbye, Teagan sat at her desk thinking about Jacob and the challenges they had faced as a couple since that amazing first night. First, there'd been Jacob's pending defamation lawsuit against Wynn. No longer an issue. The second challenge was distance, which would only become more of a problem when she moved back to Sydney. *If* she moved back. This morning she had signed an agreement to sell her business. Although she loved the people—staff as well as clients—she wasn't as sad walking away as she'd thought she might be. But the more time that passed since her last visit home, the more Teagan wondered. With her father's life no longer in danger, and Eloise making a real effort for the first time in her marriage, it didn't seem so critical to make that permanent move for the kids' sakes.

The third challenge involved trying to reconcile the legacy of Jacob's childhood with his present-day points of view. Growing up, Jacob had had it rough. Now he was a crusader for those who had been wronged, particularly by corporations—like Hunter Enterprises.

But the tipping point had come when Jacob received word that he was indeed a father. He admitted that he'd never wanted to be a parent; he certainly didn't want any more children, and he was afraid of making the same mistakes his own father had made. Teagan hadn't been able to see herself with someone who was so anti-kids...who was hardly looking forward to accepting and enjoying such a precious gift. The info Lanie had shared today hadn't convinced Teagan otherwise.

I'm sure Jacob loves that little boy...but he's so torn.

Teagan studied her screen saver—a photo of Tate cuddling Honey—and suddenly a thought came to mind.

Was she missing something—actually *two* things— that might make all the difference? She couldn't know for sure, but there was a way to find out. Of course, it would mean Jacob needing to weather another surprise, and she wasn't at all certain he would like it.

But first she had to make a decision.

Was she even brave enough to try?

Twenty

After getting Jacob's address from Lanie, Teagan flew the next morning into Connecticut, then traveled the last few miles by rental car to this house. The double-story Colonial on Huckleberry Lane wasn't scary. But the anticipation of what came next sure as heck was.

Opening the car door, Teagan reminded herself that *she* had been the one to call things off. On top of that, she and Jacob hadn't spoken in weeks. How would he react when, out of nowhere, she came knocking? Perhaps he would welcome her with open arms.

Or would he slam the door in her face?

Teagan wandered up a path that cut through a large, open yard. She had almost reached the front door—was summoning up enough nerve to ring the bell—when she heard a noise somewhere in the near distance. A low conversation.

She crossed to the side of the house and gingerly peered around the corner. Jacob was standing alongside a children's play area that housed a colorful fort, slide, swing and mini seesaw. He was shoveling from a pile of sand into a boarded-off area—filling a sandbox. His T-shirt was damp around the neck and down the back. It clung to his well-defined shoulders and biceps as he pushed the shovel in and pulled it out. He not only looked more relaxed than she remembered, he also looked *sexier*—around a thousand times more than she was prepared for.

His words were too muffled to make out. And no one else was around. So, was he talking to himself? But then he looked off toward a big elm that bookended the other side of the playground. A bouncer chair was set up under the tree's shade. A baby lay beneath the mobile animals hanging from the bouncer's handle. Every ounce of his focus was fixed upon Jacob.

On his father.

Jacob set the shovel into the sand then rested a crooked arm on the handle and wiped his brow with the sleeve of his T-shirt. He said something more and then chuckled. Oh God, she *loved* that deep rumbling sound. The baby obviously did, too; his little arms and legs started waving all over the place.

The little guy was dressed in a pale blue sleeveless onesie. Perfect for this late summer weather. His thighs were just chubby enough—so different from Honey's "lolly" legs. He had energy, too, like he wanted to leap out of that bouncer, grab a spade of his own and show Dad how it was done.

Teagan wanted to laugh. She also wanted to cry.

The scene was so ordinary and yet special. So near but also out of reach.

Jacob must have sensed someone nearby and turned around. When he saw her, he didn't move for so long, she thought he might have turned to stone.

Showtime. Deep breaths now.

Edging forward, Teagan waved in greeting.

"Hi, there."

Jacob sucked in a breath, which only inflated that amazing chest. But his expression wasn't expansive. He looked pissed. Put out.

"What are you doing here?"

Her stomach was churning. "I thought I'd drop in."

"All the way from Seattle?"

She nodded. "All the way from Seattle."

When the baby squealed, Jacob's attention whipped that way again and, in an instant, any uncertainty or aggravation dissolved from his face. With that beautiful big-cat gait, he ambled over to the bouncer, tossing his yard gloves off and wiping his brow again along the way. Then he crouched before his son and smiled like nothing else in the whole wide world mattered.

"What's up, little man?" he asked, unfastening the safety harness and scooping the baby up. "Did you see we have a guest?"

Teagan hung back. She didn't want to get in anyone's face, particularly an infant who hadn't laid eyes on her before now.

Jacob saw to the introductions. "Benson, meet Teagan."

"Pleased to meet you, Benson," she said.

The baby looked at her like Jacob had earlier—questioning, probing. But—*ohmigod!*—what about the color of his eyes? They were the exact same shade as his dad's—a mesmerizing, deep amber gold.

Teagan edged closer. "Jacob, he has your eyes."

Focused on the baby, too, Jacob gave in to a lopsided, *proud as punch* grin. "They only turned that color the last couple of weeks."

Then his brows eased together and he looked at her again. Differently this time, like he'd just remembered that six weeks ago she had left him. Goodbye forever and good luck.

His question sounded thin—like he was filling time. "How's your family?"

"Eloise seems to be cutting it in rehab."

"Hope it sticks. You know what they say about addiction. It's a hard habit to break."

She smiled. It was a joke. And it wasn't.

His lidded gaze raked over her again before he nodded toward the house. "Wanna come in for a cold drink? I have ice water."

"Ice water sounds great."

"You thirsty, too?" he asked Benson.

The baby beamed and tapped his dad's chest as if to say, *Lead the way.*

As Jacob headed off, Teagan asked, "Do you want me to carry the bouncer inside?"

He looked back and then down at the baby. "That's okay. We'll come out again later, right, Buddy?"

As they made their way across the yard, up the back stairs and into the house, Teagan couldn't fight off that sinking feeling. Lanie had said that Jacob had missed her. The vibe she was getting now was more, *Do me a favor and disappear.* On a brighter note, he didn't seem to hate being a father, and the baby certainly wasn't unhappy. Jacob had been so committed to his career. Had she caught him on a good day or was he okay with being a full-on parent every weekend?

Despite dark timber cabinetry, the large kitchen was bright—full of windows welcoming in natural light. Jacob went to the refrigerator and retrieved a yellow sippy cup. Benson put out his hands and took a small sip then another.

"He loves it cold, but not too much." When the baby pushed the cup away, Jacob added, "He's on solids now, so the digestive system's working right. Which reminds me." He crossed to a cushioned bench, lay the baby down and, like a pro, checked his diaper. "It's not good to drop off to sleep when you're wet, or worse."

When Jacob was satisfied his son was dry and clean, he scooped the baby up again and moved to a cupboard to grab a couple of glasses. With only one hand free, he got the first glass down, then the next, which he took to the refrigerator water dispenser. Teagan stepped forward. When you were carrying a baby, everyday activities weren't so easy to negotiate.

"Do you want me to take him?" Then she added, "Or I can take care of the water."

"Want to go to the nice lady?" Jacob asked Benson.

Teagan put out her hands and offered her best *this will be so much fun* look. The baby pushed out his bottom lip before he snuggled back into Jacob's arm and hid his face. Her stomach plummeted. Not a good start.

She was filling the second glass when Jacob asked, "Why are you really here, Tea?"

She hesitated before giving him the glass and the truth.

"I wanted to see if you liked being a father."

He looked…underwhelmed. Like, *I need your approval now?* Nevertheless, he asked. "How am I doing?"

"You're doing great." From what she had seen.

"I thought I'd have to think about it every minute, you know. But now, whenever Buddy and I are together, it's second nature." He winked at Benson—Buddy— who looked so gorgeous and totally at home resting against Daddy's shoulder. "Did you have any doubt?" he asked her. "Where your younger siblings were concerned, I mean."

"No doubt at all. After each one arrived, it felt as if they'd always been there, a part of our lives. I can't imagine my world without them."

"That's how I feel about Buddy. I know I was thrown by the possibility, and even more taken aback when I knew for sure he was mine. No getting around it. The news was a shock. But we're a team now. Done deal." He looked down, his eyebrows jumped, and then he chuckled. "Even if he thinks I'm a bore."

Buddy's eyes were closed, with his gorgeous little mouth slightly open and his free arm hanging. He was fast asleep and so darn cute. Teagan wanted to reach out and touch the satin of his cheek then inhale that heavenly baby scent.

She whispered, "He's really out of it."

Still gazing at his son, Jacob whispered, too. "I'll put him down. He usually naps around this time for an hour or so."

As he walked away, he lobbed a suggestion over his shoulder. "Maybe take a seat on the back porch. There's a breeze coming through."

She nodded. "Sounds good."

Still, she didn't move until Jacob had disappeared up

the staircase. That man knew how to rock a tuxedo or custom-made suit. He had blue jeans and boots down pat. But *sexy daddy putting down baby for his nap* was by far his best look. She could soak it in all day long.

She took a seat on the back porch and thought back on the conversation they had after he'd learned he was a father. He'd admitted that he had never wanted children. That he certainly didn't want any more. Some part of Jacob would always be the boy who had grown up without love or support, and he was smart enough to know that deficit could affect the relationship with his son.

The conviction behind his words that day had stopped Teagan in her tracks. His uncompromising attitude had made her think of people who complained when they heard a child cry, or rolled their eyes and shuddered if a kid was having fun rather than being "seen and not heard." She wasn't able to have one of her own, but she would always love the sound of children playing. She would always feel compassion whenever a young person was in distress or needed help. On the flip side, Jacob had thought life would be better if he never had to deal with any of it. On top of that, when she had come to the decision to call it quits for good, Jacob had bowed out without an argument. Like Damon.

But after Lanie's visit, Teagan had begun to wonder.

Despite his misgivings, could Jacob be the kind of father he had needed growing up? And if the answer to that question was yes, there was another one to ask.

How deeply did his feelings for her run? Had things become all too difficult, or were they worth fighting for? Now Teagan was more optimistic about the first question, not so confident about the second.

Jacob walked out through the back screen door. Resting his water glass on a muscular jean-clad thigh, he gazed out over the yard and playground while she took in his profile, particularly the faint smile tugging his lips.

"Buddy's in his cot." He showed her a baby monitor. "These are amazing. You can hear every peep."

"Peace of mind, huh?"

"That's the goal."

"I like his nickname."

"I got used to Benson, but he looks more like a Buddy to me. The first time I called him that, he was taking a bath. He squealed and splashed till I was soaked through."

As he brought the glass to his lips, a pulse began to beat high in his bristled cheek and then his gaze went to the porch floorboards. The pause was a long one but she waited. Obviously he had something important to say.

"There's been a new development," he finally said. "Ivy's signed over full custody."

Teagan's mouth dropped open. *What the...?*

Despite Eloise's progress, Guthrie had gone ahead and applied for sole custody of Tate and Honey, too. It was not a small thing.

"She doesn't want Buddy to live with her? Doesn't want to be involved in any of the decisions?"

Jacob shrugged one shoulder and grunted. "As of two days ago, he's all mine. She doesn't even want to visit. Says it's better this way. 'A clean cut,' she called it."

Teagan was near speechless. "I can't believe a mother would do that." Even Eloise wouldn't give her children away.

"Oh, *I* can believe it. And if that's how Ivy feels, it's better that I take over completely."

Teagan had thought that Jacob would have a hard time assimilating to part-time fatherhood. In fact, he had taken on the role *full*-time, and seemed not only committed but happy to do it.

"I'm going to have to think about how to tell Buddy one day. I don't want him growing up thinking it was his fault, because he's perfect. Everything about him."

Teagan felt the tears threatening to fall. His words and tone sealed the deal. Jacob might have his biological father's DNA but he had a mind-set and heart similar to Hux's, his dad through adoption.

"And I'm only grateful that Ivy didn't stretch it out," he went on. "At one stage, she was threatening to take me to court over some half-assed reason. What a waste of time and energy."

Teagan remembered the lawsuit Jacob had wanted to file against Wynn. Not so much fun when the shoe was on the other foot.

"So it's all done?" she asked.

"Signed and binding."

"What if Ivy changes her mind?"

His nose crinkled as he shook his head. "You'd have to know her. She had everything, anytime, in every way. Instead of understanding how lucky she was and giving back, people just don't seem to matter to her. Even her own son. Out of sight. Out of mind."

Teagan had to wonder…had Jacob been drawn to Ivy because of his past? Had he subconsciously chosen a partner who was as emotionally unavailable as his parents had been? A psychologist friend had once said that everyone wanted to recreate and control some aspect of their childhood. For example, Teagan wanted to be a wonderful parent like her own mom.

Which reminded her...

"The gym's sold," she said. "Signed the papers yesterday." She was free to return home if she wanted.

"I might have to do the same with my law firm," he said. "I can worry about having a Manhattan office after Buddy graduates. Or maybe I won't. There's lots of interesting stuff I can do from right here."

He talked about moving away from defamation cases and going into family law. He wanted to work with separated or divorced parents to get them to cooperate rather than pit one against the other. He talked about helping people with mental health and addiction problems who faced legal ramifications and family breakdown. He got particularly wound up when he explained about wanting to save as many kids as he could from juvie hell. He wanted to create a sanctuary like the Rawson Stud Farm and make certain the facility was available to boys and girls who'd been thrown away by their parents as well as society.

The longer he spoke, the more enthusiasm and belief blazed in his beautiful eyes. Teagan could have listened all day...all night.

He'd changed so much in such a short span of time. He still came across as driven but without the need to dominate. It was like he had found what made him truly happy and now he could sit back, take a breath and simply build on that.

And she got the impression he didn't see her as part of that equation. In the past, whenever they'd been together, he could barely keep from kissing her, touching her, telling her how incredible she made him feel. When she'd arrived unannounced, he'd been taken aback. Annoyed. Now it was more like, *No hard feelings*.

That left Teagan feeling like an idiot, hating that she hadn't believed in him more. Hadn't believed in *them*.

Jacob checked his wristwatch. "I should wake Buddy up. If he sleeps too long during the day, he wants to stay up and play with the owls."

"Does he have a cuddle toy?"

"*Cuddle toy?* I would say no."

"I've read that can help for babies over six, seven months old. Around that age, they become aware of separation. Having a familiar face in the cot can be a comfort."

He was nodding. "Sure. I'll pick one up this week." He cast a look out toward that elm and pushed to his feet. "Better put away that shovel and bring the bouncer in. He's probably had enough of the outdoors for one day."

Was that code for wanting her to hang around a bit longer? Or was she overthinking it? Should she tell him how she felt or bow out gracefully now? This all felt so different to what she'd imagined.

He sauntered across the lawn and scooped up the shovel. Then he inspected the sandbox again before disappearing into the big backyard and ducking through some shrubs, which she presumed hid a shed. Watching his every move, Teagan was left feeling a little giddy. In her eyes, he would always be the sexiest man alive, the person who could make her tingle with just a look. And whenever they kissed…whenever they touched…

If they made love now, would it be the same?

Or would it be better?

Suddenly the baby monitor went off. Buddy wasn't just shifting on his cot up there, or even fussing as he woke up. What Teagan heard was a piercing scream that lifted her out of her shoes.

Fumbling, she snatched the monitor up and checked the video feed. Buddy was standing in his cot—*he was old enough to do that?*—holding on to the rail, his gorgeous little face all puckered up. She called toward the shrubs.

"Jacob! *Jacob!*"

Buddy was crying now. *Really* crying. Teagan whimpered, dropped the monitor and bolted inside.

As she ran through the kitchen, an obvious question dawned. Buddy's bedroom was upstairs, but which one was it? As she raced up the stairs, she realized she only needed to follow the wails.

Still standing in the cot, the baby had one arm flung out like he was trying to snatch a rope. Teagan raced over and, without thinking, scooped him out and into her arms.

"It's okay, Buddy. I'm here. Your daddy's coming, too." She threw a glance at the open bedroom door. "Soon. He'll be here really, really soon."

The baby was nestled upright against her chest, his little chin on her shoulder. The motion she used was a cross between rocking and jostling, a fast jigging movement meant to distract as much as soothe.

Hurry up, Jacob. Hurry the heck up!

But of course she could take Buddy downstairs. Right now. No big deal.

Then she realized the baby had stopped crying. *Completely.* Teagan was almost too scared to look; she didn't want to get him started again.

Slowly she lowered him from her shoulder and held him a little away from her. His face was all red. His cheeks were wet. Watching her now, he didn't smile, but at least he didn't scream again.

That's when Jacob swept into the room like there was a fire. He pulled up sharp and ran a hand down his face. Finally, he smiled.

"Well, I see you two have gotten better acquainted."

"Sorry." She shrugged. "We couldn't wait."

And now that Jacob was here, naturally Buddy would want to go to his dad.

But the baby only kept his gaze on Teagan, like she was some strange curiosity. And while he stared, he clung to her blouse, gently tugging the fabric one way, then the other. She caught their reflection in the windowpane. Weird, but not. The image of her and this baby, with Daddy in the background, reminded her of a family photo.

Joining them, Jacob dropped a kiss on his son's crown. Then he looked at Teagan like she might actually be an asset.

"How are you with giving baby baths?"

"I'm…pretty good, actually."

"Are you available? Or are you on a time line?"

"I haven't booked a flight back yet."

"Well, I'm planning steak for dinner. Mashed veggies for Buddy—if you'd like to stay?"

Lifting her chin, she started putting together a proper response in her mind. But poise didn't count now. This wasn't the time to play it cool.

"I'd like that, Jacob," she said. "I'd like that very much."

Twenty-One

Teagan watched while Jacob gave Buddy his bath.

He was spot-on making sure all the creases and fiddly bits like ears were attended to. When he tickled his son's belly with the washcloth, she laughed along with the baby. And after Jacob had dried him and applied baby powder, she was gobsmacked at the expertise with which he managed the diaper. It was that *sexy baby daddy* thing again. *So* attractive.

But it was more than that. The way Jacob cared for his child touched her so very deeply. It made her feel wistful but also hopeful, particularly whenever he wanted her to join in.

"You seem to have all the baby stuff down pat," she said as they headed downstairs to start on dinner.

"I read a couple of books on basics and got hooked on *You're a New Daddy* videos. If you know a few tricks, it's pretty smooth sailing. Helps when you have a good kid."

Heading into the kitchen, he rubbed his forehead against Buddy's. The baby giggled like he'd heard the world's funniest joke. No one learned *that* from a book or video. Despite earlier misgivings, it seemed Jacob was a natural and Buddy loved him all the more for it.

Jacob set Buddy up in a nearby playpen with some toys while they got to work cooking. Again, she was impressed. In between chopping and marinating and mashing, he talked about time-saving techniques, how he stayed clear of preservatives and food coloring where Buddy was concerned, and how he was going to try out a new spaghetti sauce recipe next week.

The way to a man's heart was supposedly through his stomach. Now she put her own spin on the adage. The way to *her* heart was watching Jacob master this new domain. On the side, she fantasized about seeing him go about things wearing nothing but an apron.

Which, of course, led to thinking about later when Buddy was asleep and they were alone. Not that she wished this time away. She was enjoying every single moment. She wished it would never end.

When dinner was served, Buddy was set up next to his dad in a high chair. Jacob spoon-fed him some mashed veggies, which he devoured. When he'd had enough, Jacob attached a set of toy keys to the tray to keep him amused while the adults ate. Too easy.

After stacking the dinner dishes on the counter—Teagan had said she would load the dishwasher when Jacob took Buddy to bed—they sat together in the living room. Jacob talked on about all the different things Buddy could do.

"His first word was *buba*," Jacob said, holding Buddy on his lap while the baby gnawed a corner of a plastic book about jungle animals. "Then *Dada*. No coaching."

As if to confirm the point, Buddy said, *"Dada. Dada,"* before going back to chewing. Clever. But his eyelids were drooping now. Then came a yawn.

By the time Jacob had dimmed the lights and read him the book, pointing out and describing all the pictures, Buddy was ready to go down for the night. Teagan wiggled her fingers and singsonged, "Night-night, Buddy," before Jacob took him up to bed.

Watching them go, Teagan told herself again how wrong she had been to prejudge. Jacob was patient with Buddy, and good-humored and kind. He literally *shone* as a father. The real joy was how much they both so obviously loved being together.

Was there room enough for her to visit again? After that shaky start today, was there any hope that Jacob might still feel the same way he had about her? Since the baby monitor incident, he'd included her in things, but there hadn't been the slightest hint of romance. Nothing in his eyes that spoke to a need to take her in his arms. But after Buddy was put down for the night, perhaps they could discuss the second reason she had come.

Did Jacob care about her still? Or had she literally thrown *them* away?

By the time Jacob got upstairs, Buddy was already asleep. As he laid a light cover over his son, he deliberated more on Teagan's surprise visit today. No phone call, no warning, no, *Sorry I didn't believe in you and dropped your sorry ass cold*. Was he being too harsh or did she have a nerve?

Making his way back downstairs, he wondered how best to convey his feelings on the subject now that there was little chance of them being interrupted. Perhaps, *Thanks for taking the time, now excuse me while Buddy and I get on with our lives*. Like Teagan was getting on with hers. With the gym sold, she would soon be jetting off to rejoin her billionaire clan on the other side of the world. Cool. She had her family and, you'd better believe, he had his.

He'd even met someone who had let him know he was doing a good job. Someone who thought Buddy was the absolute best. A woman they both could trust.

Jacob found Teagan where he'd left her. Sitting on the couch, she was thumbing through Buddy's book, looking hauntingly beautiful beneath the lights' soft glow. These past weeks, he'd thought about her way too much…her hair, her scent, most of all her touch. But when people let you down, you dusted yourself off and moved on. You survived…even when something fierce and deep inside clawed at you to hold on.

When she looked across and smiled, Jacob bit down against the almighty tug in his gut. They had a history in the bedroom like nothing he had experienced before. But the tender moments they had shared were even more memorable. Watching her sleep, hearing her laugh, holding her extra close just because.

"Buddy's down?" she asked as he walked over. "That didn't take long."

"He should sleep through the night."

She sighed. "He's just so sweet."

Yep. "I know."

Her eyebrows knitted as she put the book aside. "I can't understand his mother…"

"You mean about her not giving a crap?" He sat down. "I understand her perfectly."

Teagan's eyes filled with pity. "Because of your own mother?"

"That woman was so out of it, she didn't care whether I lived or died." Thinking of Buddy again, he growled and shook his head. "Sometimes I feel like I handed down some twisted family curse."

"It's not your fault Ivy Schluter has no heart."

"But I did make the choice to be with her." To *sleep* with her.

"And now you have a beautiful son." Her gaze grew distant as she murmured, "I always wanted kids of my own."

"I never wanted to be a parent, period."

She blinked and then straightened. "That's why I thought we wouldn't work out, Jacob. Why I decided it was best we didn't see each other again."

"And, frankly, I think you were right."

She froze before visibly composing herself. "I didn't know how you would cope with being a father."

"Sure." He shrugged. "Easier to opt out."

Her jaw dropped. "That's not fair."

"Life's not fair."

He didn't like saying it. He liked less the look on her face. But, *Sorry not sorry*. That was God's honest truth.

She was getting to her feet. "I shouldn't have come here."

"So, why did you?"

"Because…" She paused then squared her shoulders. "Because I couldn't forget you."

"I see." Churning inside, he stood, too. "You needed another fix."

Her nostrils flared as the corners of her beautiful mouth turned down. "Now you're being cruel."

He was being cruel? Wow. She really had no idea.

"We were always somehow out of sync," she added.

Jacob's chest was so tight now, it ached. But he kept his voice even. His emotions under control.

"It doesn't matter anymore."

"No," she agreed. "I guess not."

So—*over*. Done. No need to shake hands, remain friends, drag this drama out any further.

But she was looking at him with such intensity, like *her* conclusion was something else entirely. Like maybe they'd just had a lover's spat and she was waiting for the making up part to begin. And in that moment, with his heart blocking his throat and all that pent up stuff off his chest, a pragmatic part of him felt almost willing to listen, and even to goad.

It wasn't as if anyone's life would be irreparably shattered come morning.

He took a step closer. When she drew a breath then did the same, the energy crackling between them flashed and caught fire.

Focusing on her lips, he lowered his voice.

"You didn't answer my question."

"About needing a fix?" Her eyes glistened as she shrugged. "Maybe it's that simple, Jacob. Maybe I'm addicted."

He almost winced, but the language fit. This minute he needed her that much, too. More than he was prepared to ever let her know.

Threading his fingers up through the back of her hair,

he enjoyed watching her limpid eyes darken and those lips quiver then part. And when his mouth claimed hers and she melted against him—when she clung on to his shirt and whimpered in her throat—Jacob embraced the sense of power mixed with relief. He hadn't planned for this to happen, but this coming together would be different from anything they had shared before. This was purely physical. Entirely sexual.

One more fix.

One last time.

Twenty-Two

Teagan woke up with a start.

When she realized where she was—when she remembered in a flash what had happened—she grinned from ear to ear and stretched like a cat. But how long had she been lying here alone?

Last night, after Buddy had gone to bed, the adults had a hard-hitting conversation where painful truths were hashed out. Jacob had been exceptionally blunt and she'd gotten justifiably upset. But underpinning it all had been a reality neither one could deny. No matter how much they disagreed, the attraction they felt for each other only seemed to grow stronger, deeper.

Hotter.

When he had finally kissed her, she practically dissolved. In no time, they were in this guest bedroom, sans clothes and regrets. Afterward, curling up against all that amazing masculine heat, she had clocked out and fallen fast asleep.

Big day.

Now, still feeling as though she were in a dream, she slipped out of bed and into the attached bathroom. She had an overnight bag stowed away in the rental car, but for now she was happy to hurry back into yesterday's clothes. She couldn't wait to find Jacob and talk more because now she was certain. This time there was no turning back.

She was in love with Jacob Stone. More than that, after their day spent together with Buddy and then last night, she was looking forward to spending the future with them both. She'd never felt so sure about anything in her life. In her heart, she knew he felt the same way.

She found him in the kitchen, standing at a counter, laptop open. After rushing both hands through her un-brushed hair, she strode over.

"Guess I overslept," she said with a big smile.

Shifting his focus from the laptop, Jacob looked across. She expected his gorgeous eyes to gleam with approval. She thought a bold grin would instantly light up his face.

Instead, he studied her with a laid-back kind of curiosity. Almost like he'd forgotten about last night. Like he'd forgotten she was even there.

"I just put Buddy down for his morning nap." He made a move toward the percolator. "Want a coffee?"

Teagan shook herself and held up a hand. "Uh… I can get it."

After he nodded and went back to his laptop, Teagan tried to gather her thoughts while she found a cup and poured. Had she woken up in an alternate universe? Because last night had definitely happened. Her body still tingled. Her lips still burned. But what they had shared was way more than mind-blowing sex. It was about an understanding. An irreversible coming together.

Cradling her cup, she joined him by the counter. He smelled so good—fresh out of the shower with hints of his natural scent. His hair was still damp and a pulse was beating in his unshaven jaw. She wanted to lean in and graze her lips over the spot. She wanted to tell him how happy she felt now that everything was good.

But his attention remained fixed to the screen.

She tried to make a joke. "Looking into colleges for Buddy?"

"I'm searching out community organizations around here. Thinking more about moving on from Lexington Avenue." His eyes narrowed, like he was thinking back. "When did you say you were heading back to Sydney?"

Teagan hesitated and then smiled. That must be the reason he was acting so strange. He didn't know.

"Actually," she said, "that was something I wanted to talk to you about."

His brows nudged together as his chin came down. "Has something happened? Are the kids okay?"

"Considering everything that's gone on, they're actually doing really well. Honey's put on weight, and I Skype with Tate all the time."

"So, what's the problem?"

She tried to explain. "These past few months, Dad wasn't the only one in danger. We older kids passed the baton, doing our best to keep Tate, and later Honey, out of harm's way. We all felt we needed to be there when we could. But that danger's definitely over now. Dad and Eloise still have issues to work through, but that's really their business, not mine."

He seemed to soak that in before changing the subject, like what she'd just said didn't naturally lead into another conversation—about *them*.

"Are you hungry?" he asked, moving to a cupboard. "I could whip up some pancakes."

Teagan's stomach knotted. "I don't want pancakes, Jacob. I want to talk."

His mouth pulled to one side as he sized her up. "Talk about what?"

She coughed out a humorless laugh. "Are you serious? You're acting like nothing happened last night."

He scratched his temple. "How do you want me to act?"

That really took her aback. Was he gaslighting or had she truly gone mad?

"Jacob, are you saying that being together again didn't mean anything to you?"

"I'm saying you made the decision for us weeks ago."

"I explained—"

"You made a choice," he cut in. "I made a choice, too." His gaze narrowed. "I have my son to think about now."

A knock on the front door interrupted them. Jacob blinked before his attention shot that way. Then he checked the time on his wristwatch.

"I'm expecting someone," he said.

Teagan tried to gather her whirling thoughts. What he'd said, how he'd acted…it had taken her completely off guard. Cut her to the quick. But his reasons for putting up this wall made perfect sense. Yes, she had made a choice, which meant when he had really needed her support, she'd stepped away. Shutting her out now probably wasn't so much about *him* being hurt as it was about protecting Buddy.

The same way, not so long ago, she had needed to protect Tate.

Getting a second wind, Teagan followed him. She needed Jacob to know that after he'd taken care of whoever was at the door, they should talk again. These past weeks had been a roller coaster ride, but they were smoothing out all the humps now. This was a long way from over.

Jacob had opened the door. A woman stood on the other side of the threshold—around Teagan's age, with ice-blond hair, wearing modest shorts matched with a midriff shirt. She was naturally pretty in a fresh-faced, *girl next door* kind of way.

And Jacob was expecting her...why?

"Hope you don't mind that I'm early." All smiles, the woman stepped inside. Then her gaze met Teagan's and her expression changed while Teagan's heart missed a few beats.

Jacob looked between the two women before he rolled back his shoulders and stepped back. "Monica, this is Teagan."

Monica's eyes widened before she sent a frown Jacob's way. Teagan imagined the other woman's expression said, *What the hell is she doing here?*

At that moment, baby noises trickled down from upstairs. Monica didn't hesitate. She stepped around Jacob, already on her way.

"Can I go get him?"

Teagan thought of how she had raced to Buddy yesterday when she had heard him cry out on the baby monitor. But Monica obviously didn't need to think about which room. She wasn't worried about Buddy being wary of a new face.

Jacob sent Monica a smile. "Sure. Go up."

While Monica flew up the stairs, Jacob stuck his hands in his jeans' back pockets and met Teagan's gaze. He was waiting for questions, but his silence was all the response she needed. *I made a choice, too*.

Feeling her cheeks burn and her heart drop, she asked, "Who is she?"

His gaze held hers. "I thought that would be obvious."

The backs of her eyes were suddenly prickling with tears. They had slept together when he was seeing another woman? And to think she was ready to trust this guy.

Teagan had left her handbag by the couch. Now Jacob watched as she moved to collect the bag and walk out the door without another look or a word. Rather than see her stride down the path to her car parked on the street, he forced himself to shut the door and turn away.

Monica had started down the stairs with Buddy in her arms. Before Jacob could open his mouth, she got in first.

"You don't have to explain," she said.

He had mentioned Teagan to Monica once in a weak moment. He could admit that he hadn't painted her in a very good light.

"She showed up yesterday out of the blue," he said.

"None of my business," Mon replied. "I'm just the nanny."

Not *just a nanny*. Mon did a fantastic job. He and Buddy had been damn lucky to find her.

Jacob cupped his son's flushed cheek. And when Buddy put out his arms, despite feeling like shit, Daddy found a bigger smile and took him in a heartbeat.

"He'll want a bottle," Monica said. "I can put his

laundry on while it heats up." She paused. "Or, if you don't need me today after all, that's fine. We're still working this out."

After learning that he would have Buddy full-time, Jacob had pulled out all the stops to find a nanny whom he and Buddy could trust. The agency had put Monica's application forward. She was back in the area, staying with her folks after a stint working in orphanages overseas. Her credentials were impeccable and her easy way with Buddy had won both father and son over in no time. She was staying for perhaps six months in the district before moving on again. He didn't want to lose her while he searched for someone more permanent.

He hadn't mentioned her to Teagan because—why? He had assumed that she would be gone, well on her way, before Monica showed up today—earlier than expected, as it turned out. No one could accuse Mon of being tardy. She had their best interests at heart.

Taking a seat on the couch, he set Buddy on his lap and let the nanny know, "Everything's sorted out. We're all set."

Still, Monica slid a questioning look toward the door before walking away.

While the baby played with the hairs on his arm and blew bubbles, Jacob talked to him. He did it a lot. Maybe too much. But Buddy never seemed to mind, and, after that horror of a scene, his dad could sure use a sympathetic ear.

"Teagan mustn't think too much of me. Hey, I'm far from *my* favorite person right now. I know she hurt me, probably more than I've ever been hurt before, and that's saying a lot. But I shouldn't have done what I did. I swore I'd always be honest, no matter what, and I *lied* to her. I let her believe we could go back to how it was. But you can never go back, Buddy. The only way is forward, and in our case that means you and me. A tandem team cooking with gas. We don't need anyone else because going that route…" He winced. "It's just too darn hard. Feeling for someone, laying your heart on the line, worrying about when the next bombshell will land. Not that all surprises turn out to be bad. Not when you get used to the idea."

Jacob tickled his son's belly, which drew a giggle. God, he loved this kid. Would die for him in a heartbeat.

"Some of life's biggest challenges," Jacob went on, "can turn out to be blessings in disguise when you can drill down on what's most important. On what you really want and need and cherish, even when you know there will always be more challenges ahead, because anything worthwhile requires work and trust and—"

Jacob bit down as his chest tightened and his gut wrenched.

"God, I really let her go, didn't I? I seriously just let Teagan believe the absolute worst and walk away."

"She's still out front by her car."

Jacob's head snapped up. Monica was back from the laundry and headed over.

"I don't think she can find her keys," she said, taking Buddy when the baby put out his arms to her. "I was going out to check if she was okay." Mon gave a knowing smile. "But I thought you might want to do that."

The damn key had to be here somewhere. But the more Teagan burrowed around in her purse, the more her face burned and she wanted to fall apart. Soon enough that car key would appear. Then she could jump inside that vehicle and keep driving until this nightmare of a morning was nothing more than a sickening memory.

Jacob Stone. She never wanted to hear his name again. She needed to wipe away every thought she'd ever formed around him, particularly the ones seared into her brain from last night when she'd fallen like a sap into his arms again.

As a tear escaped and rolled down her cheek, Teagan set her jaw and cursed under her breath.

Why had she ever thought that coming here was a good idea? Wynn had it right from the start. Jacob was a first-class manipulator who couldn't be trusted. He had taken her to bed when he was already seeing someone else—a woman who obviously had no problems with slotting in with this *eligible single dad* lifestyle.

Well, good luck to her, Teagan thought, dumping the contents of her bag on the hood and wincing at the screechy-clatter of lipstick, cell phone and every other damn thing hitting the metal. Good luck, and good riddance, to them all.

Suddenly the key was there, staring back at her. She snatched at the tag, but it somehow slipped under her hand and fell between the tire and the curb. Cursing again, she got down and fished the key out. When she straightened, he was there, looking even more infuriatingly sexy than he had five minutes ago.

"You had trouble finding your key," Jacob said, like she didn't know that already.

Her face was damp with tears, but she wouldn't give him the satisfaction of seeing her wipe them away. And she didn't feel the need to respond, either, other than to turn her back on him. She didn't need his help. She didn't need him, period.

She pressed the remote and the doors beeped open. But then she remembered the handbag stash still strewn all over the hood. As she scooped everything back into her bag, Jacob opened the driver's side door.

Geez, what a gentleman.

"That woman," he said. "Monica—"

"I don't want to know," she replied, pushing around him to get inside.

"I know what you're thinking," he went on, "but you're wrong. Mon is Buddy's nanny."

Teagan stopped dead. Then she scowled and shook her head. That woman did not look like a nanny.

Then again, Dex's fiancée, Shelby, didn't look like Mary Poppins, either.

"This morning I didn't want you to think that I cared anymore," he said. "But I was trying to convince *myself* more than anyone else." His eyes flashed in the sunshine as he edged closer. "But I *do* care, Tea. I care a lot. In fact, I really need to tell you just how much."

Teagan put up a hand and shut her eyes tight. "I don't need to listen to any of this."

But being the overbearing man that he was, he told her anyway.

"The truth is, I'm in love with you. I've never said that to anyone before. But saying it now, knowing that it's real…" His mouth kicked up at one side. "I can't believe how good it feels."

When the shock subsided, Teagan pushed him hard in the ribs. Then she pushed him again.

"Don't you dare do that," she said. "Don't for a minute think you can play with me that way."

As if what he'd already done wasn't enough.

"I've never been more serious in my life." He held her

arms and stepped into the space separating them. "When I saw you yesterday, I didn't want to let myself feel that way again. I didn't want to set myself up for another fall. But when we finally got to be alone and things started to happen, of course I wanted to be with you." His grip on her arms tightened. "Like I want to be with you now."

Teagan suddenly felt so weak. So confused. "That's not what you said a few minutes ago."

"I didn't want to risk being hurt again. But it's way scarier to think about my life without you. Without your smile and your strength and your love."

Her breath caught in her throat and grew into a lump.

"I never said that I loved you."

Cocking his head, he grinned. "Not yet."

She pulled back. "I'm sorry I hurt you, but, Jacob, you hurt me, too."

"So why don't we be grown-ups and just forgive each other?"

She thought about it. "And then what?"

"Then we start again. Start afresh."

Her stomach was a hot knotted mess. But he looked so certain. So…ready.

She bit her lip and almost smiled. "You really think we can?"

"I *know* we can. And one reason is the cute kid inside that house who is dying to have a mom he can depend on."

Her heart was bursting.

"Me?" she squeaked.

His answer was to bring her close at the same time his mouth captured hers with a kiss that turned her blood into molten lava and her heart into mush. And as the kiss deepened and she felt his strength wrap around her, any lingering doubts she might have had evaporated beneath the steam.

When he gradually broke the kiss, he brushed his smile over her lips.

"I love you, Tea. And that will never change. Never die."

Teagan thought about her life ahead with a man she loved so much, too, and with an adorable child who would actually, truly be hers. When her eyes filled again, this time she didn't want to wipe the tears away. Sometimes people cried because they were happy, and she had never been happier in her life.

When he rested his brow against hers, waiting for her answer, she let out a grateful sigh. "This is real— isn't it?"

Before he kissed her again, Jacob promised her with all his heart. "This is the way it's going to be. Us together. A family forever. That's the truth, Tea, so help me God."

* * * * *

*If you loved Jacob's story,
you won't want to miss
his brother Ajax Rawson!*

One Night with His Rival
by Robyn Grady

*Available March 2020
from Harlequin Desire*

WE HOPE YOU ENJOYED THIS BOOK!

HARLEQUIN® *Desire*

Experience sensual stories of juicy drama and intense chemistry cast in the world of the American elite.

Discover six new books every month, available wherever books are sold!

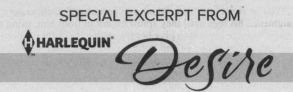
"Do we know each other?"

Her sharp but low intake of breath glanced off his ears, and he
faced her again, openly scrutinizing her face for any telltale signs of
deception. But she was good. Aside from that gasp, her expression
remained shuttered. Either she had nothing to hide or she was damn
good at lying.

He couldn't decide which one to believe.

"No," she whispered. "We don't know each other."

Truth rang in her voice, and the vise squeezing his chest loosened
a fraction of an inch.

"And I guess I didn't see the point of exchanging names. If not
for this blackout or you being in this hallway instead of the ballroom,
our paths wouldn't have crossed. And when the power is restored,
we'll become strangers again. Getting to know each other will pass
the time, but it's not because we truly want to. It's not...honest."

Her explanation struck him like a punch. It echoed throughout his
body, vibrating through skin and bone. Honest. What did he know
about that?

In the world he moved in, deception was everywhere—from the
social niceties of "It's so good to see you" to the cagey plans to land
a business deal. He wasn't used to her brand of frankness, and so he
didn't give her platitudes. Her honesty deserved more than that.

"You're right," he said. "And you're wrong." Deliberately, he straightened his legs until they sprawled out in front him, using that moment to force himself to give her the truth. "If not for me needing to get out of that ballroom and bumping into you here, we wouldn't have met. You would be outside, unprotected in the parking lot or on the road. And I would be trapped in the dark with people I wish I didn't know, most likely going out of my mind. So for that alone, I'm glad we did connect. Because, Nadia…" He surrendered to the need that had been riding him since looking down into her upturned face and clasped a lock of her hair, twisting it around his finger. "Nadia, I would rather be out here with you, a complete stranger I've met by serendipity, than surrounded by the familiar strangers I've known for years in that ballroom."

She stared at him, her pretty lips slightly parted, eyes widened in surprise.

"Another thing you're correct and incorrect about. True, when the lights come back on and we leave here, we probably won't see each other again. But in this moment, there's nothing I want more than to discover more about Nadia with the gorgeous mouth and the unholy curves."

Maybe he shouldn't have pushed it with the comments about her mouth and body, but if they were being truthful, then he refused to hide how attractive he found her. Attractive, hell. Such an anemic description for his hunger to explore every inch of her and be able to write a road map later.

Her lashes fluttered before lowering, hiding her eyes. In her lap, her elegant fingers twisted. He released the strands of her hair and checked the impulse to tip her chin up and order her to look at him.

"Why did you need to escape the ballroom?" she asked softly.

He didn't immediately reply, instead waiting until her gaze rose to meet his.

Only then did he whisper, "To find you."

Find out what happens next in
Blame It on the Billionaire
by USA TODAY *bestselling author Naima Simone.*

Available February 2020 wherever
Harlequin® Desire books and ebooks are sold.

Harlequin.com